THE
SINGULARITY

Issue 2

The Singularity

2

Editor-in-Chief: Lee P. Hogg

Editor: Tim Major

First Readers: Matt King and Tim Major

Proofreaders: Matt King and Sarah Lucas

Cover Art by Christoph Struber

www.thesingularitymagazine.com

ISBN: 152289781X
ISBN 13: 978-1522897811

Contents

Editorial

Following the launch of the first ever issue of *The Singularity*, and after receiving a warm and positive response, we now return for Issue 2. Like the first, it includes ten singular pieces of fiction from some of the biggest names to newly published writers, from our shores, across the pond and right around the world.

In this issue, we have the story "Monsters" by one of the leading speculative writers in the UK, Chris Beckett. His exceptional work *Dark Eden*, for which he won the Arthur C. Clarke Award in 2013, is a fantastic read and if you haven't had the opportunity to read it yet, I urge you to do so. Like all of his stories, "Monsters" is acutely socially perceptive and an excellent read. We also have the original story "Blindr (Beta 3.1)" from Rich Larson. Rich now frequently appears in all of the major American and Canadian publications, and it's a pleasure to feature his singularly breakneck prose in the magazine. We also have the story "Three Brother Cities", by Deborah Walker, that resonates like an Ursula K. Le Guin tale, a magical fable in "Mynah for the King" by Ahmed A. Khan, and "Memory Walk" from the Wendy S. Delmater – Editor-in-Chief of the valued *Abyss and Apex* magazine. "The Stupefying Snailman, Gastropod of Justice versus The Disease that Steals the Soul" by Ira Nayman – our first author writing from Down Under, "Another Reboot" by Russ Bickerstaff, and "Pipes" by Margaret Karmazin. Finally, we are pleased to feature two previously unpublished authors in Steve Jarratt and Steve Pease, with their stories "Chances" and "Commemoration of the Faithful Departed" respectively. All in all, I think it makes for a rich and distinct flavour to the issue.

As you will have already seen, we have another wonderful piece of cover art, *The Artefact,* from Christoph Struber. Christoph, like many of our contributors, has been extremely enthusiastic about the magazine and I'd like to thank him again for providing the cover art for this one.

Just a quick reminder to say that, at present, we are still open for fiction and cover art submissions. Also, a quick mention that we now have a donation button on our website. We want to pay our richly deserving authors and artists, and your support will help make this happen and provide a long-term future for the magazine. I would like to give a massive thank you to those who have contributed already – you really are what the speculative fiction community is all about.

I hope you enjoy the magazine as much as we've enjoyed creating it. Until next time . . .

Lee P. Hogg

The Artefact
Christoph Struber

CHRISTOPH STRUBER (aka dadrian) is an Austrian visual effects artist living in Germany. He has started with Space Art in High School because planets are circles and circles are easy to draw with a computer. CGI is his greatest hobby so he has studied Digital Media. Now he does effects for movies and commercials for a living. Chris has written his master's thesis on Space Opera, so it comes as no surprise that he is a huge nerd and SF lover. He spends the summer in the famous Munich beer gardens and the winter skiing in the Austrian mountains. In between he tries to read all the classic science fiction novels. Space Art has always stayed a personal hobby and the DeviantArt Space Art community is his home in the net.

Monsters
Chris Beckett

"This is Dirk Johns, our leading novelist," said the poet's mother, "and this is Lucille, who makes wonderful little landscapes out of clay . . ."

"Oh, just decorative," protested the novelist's tiny, bird-like wife, "purely decorative and nothing more."

"And this is Angelica Meadows, the painter. You perhaps caught her recent exhibition in the Metropolis, Mr Clancy? I believe it received very good notices."

"I believe I did hear something . . ." I lied, shaking hands with a very attractive young woman with lively, merry eyes. "I'm afraid I spend so little time in the Metropolis these days."

"And this," went on the poet's mother, "is the composer, Ulrika Bennett. We expect great things of her."

No, I thought, looking into Ulrika Bennett's cavernous eyes, great music will never come from you. You are too intense. You lack the necessary playfulness.

And then there was Ulrika's husband, "the ceramicist", and then an angry little dramatist, and then a man who uncannily resembled a tortoise, complete with wrinkled neck, bald head and tiny pursed little mouth.

"Well," I said, "I'm honoured."

The tortoise was, it seemed, "our foremost conductor and the director of our national conservatory."

"The honour is ours, Mr Clancy," he said. "We have all read your extraordinary books, even out here."

~~~

"William!" called the poet's mother, "let us lead the way to dinner!"

The poet turned from a conversation with the painter Angelica. He had wonderfully innocent blue eyes, which had the odd quality that, while they seemed terribly naked and vulnerable, they were simultaneously completely opaque.

"Yes, of course, Mother."

He pushed her wheelchair through into the panelled dining room and the guests took their seats. I was given the head of the table. William sat at the opposite end, his mother by his side. Servants brought in the soup.

"William and I are trying hard," announced the poet's mother to the whole company, "to persuade Mr Clancy that there is more to our little colony than cattle ranches."

"Indeed," I said soothingly, "there is clearly also a thriving cultural life which I would very much like to hear more about."

Well, they needed no second bidding. *Remarkable* things were being achieved under the circumstances, I was told, for the arts were struggling by with an *appalling* lack of support. Apart from the poet's mother, Lady Henry, who was of course *wonderful*, there was not a single serious patron of the fine arts to be found in the whole of Flain. Everyone present did their heroic best, of course, but not one of them had achieved the recognition that their talents deserved . . .

And so on. I had heard it many times before, in many more provincial outposts than I cared to remember. I made my usual sympathetic noises.

It was as the dessert was being served that I became aware of the poet's blue eyes upon me.

"Tell me honestly, Mr Clancy," he asked – and at once his mother was listening intently, as if she feared he would need rescuing from himself – "had you heard of even *one* of us here in this room, before you knew you were coming to Flain?"

I hadn't, honestly, and from what little I had seen of their outmoded and derivative efforts, it was not surprising. (Let's face it, even in the Metropolis, for every hundred who fancy themselves as artists, there is only one who has anything interesting to say. It is just that in the Metropolis, even one per cent is still a good many gifted and interesting people.)

But before I could frame a suitably tactful reply, William's mother had intervened.

"Really, William, how rude!"

"Rude?" His face was innocence itself. "Was that rude? I do apologise. Then let me ask you another question instead, Mr Clancy. What in particular were you hoping to see on your visit here? Please don't feel you *have* to mention our artistic efforts."

"Well I'm interested in every aspect of course," I replied. "But I don't deny that I'd like to learn more about the fire horses."

There was a noticeable drop of temperature in the room and everyone's eyes turned to Lady Henry, watching for her reaction.

"Fire horses," sighed the novelist, Johns. "Of course. The first thing every Metropolitan wants to see. Yet surely you must have them in zoos there?"

I shrugged.

"Of course, but then we have *everything* in the Metropolis, everything remotely interesting that has ever existed anywhere. I travel to see things in context. And fire horses *are* Flain to the outside world, the thing which makes Flain unique. It was wonderful when I first disembarked here to see boys with their young fire horses playing in the streets."

"How I wish the brutes had been wiped out by the first colonists," said the poet's mother. "Your curiosity is perfectly understandable, Mr Clancy, but this country will not progress until we are known for something other than one particularly ugly and ferocious animal."

"Yes," I said, soothingly, "I *do* see that it must be irritating when one's homeland always conjures up the same one thing in the minds of outsiders."

"It *is* irritating to think that our country is known only for its monsters," said Lady Henry, "but unfortunately it is more than just irritating. How will we ever develop anything approaching a mature and serious cultural life as long as the educated and uneducated alike spend all their free time yelling their heads off in horse-races and horse-fights, and a man's worth is measured in equestrian skill? I do not blame you for your curiosity, Mr Clancy, but how we *long* for visitors who come with something other than fire horses in mind."

"Hear, hear," said several of them, but the poet smiled and said nothing.

"Well, I'll have to see what I can do about that," I said.

7

But of course in reality I knew that my Metropolitan readers would not be any more interested than I was in the arch theatricals at the Flain Opera or the third-rate canvasses in the National Gallery of Flain, straining querulously for profundity and importance. 'The Arts' are an urban thing, after all, and no one does urban things better than the Metropolis itself.

"I hardly like to mention it," I said in a humble voice, which I hoped would be disarming, "but the other thing for which Flain is famous is of course the game of sky-ball."

The poet's mother gave a snort of distaste.

"Ritualised thuggery!" she exclaimed. "And so tedious. I can't abide the game myself. I honestly think I would rather watch paint drying on a wall. I really do. At least it would be restful."

But Angelica the painter took a different view.

"Oh I *love* sky-ball!" she declared. "There's a big game tomorrow – the Horsemen and the Rockets. William and I should take you there, Mr Clancy. You'll have a wonderful time!"

William smiled.

"Good idea, Angie. I'd be very glad to take you, Mr Clancy, if you'd like to go."

"But Mr Clancy is to visit the Academy tomorrow," protested his mother. "Professor Hark himself has agreed to show him round. We really cannot . . ."

"I do *so* appreciate the trouble you've gone to," I purred, "but if it is at *all* possible to put Professor Hark off, I would very much like to see the Horsemen and the Rockets."

For, even back in the Metropolis, I had heard of the Horsemen and the Rockets.

"Well, of course," said Lady Henry, "if you want to go to the game we must take you. You know best what you need to see. I will talk to Professor Hark. No, a sky-ball game will be . . . an experience for me."

"But good Lord, Lady Henry" I protested, "there's no need for you to come if you don't want. I'm sure William and Miss Meadows and I can . . ."

Polite murmurs of support came from the distinguished guests, but Lady Henry was resolved:

"Don't be ridiculous, Mr Clancy, of course I will come. We must sample every aspect of life, must we not? Not just those we find congenial." She summoned up a brave smile. "No, I am sure it will be *great fun.*"

~~~

So we set off in the Henrys' car the next morning, Lady Henry riding up in front next to the elderly chauffeur (the seat had been removed to accommodate her wheelchair) while William and myself reclined on red leather in the back. We picked up Angelica on the way and she squeezed in between us, warm and alive and smelling of freshly mowed grass.

"I do hope you don't support the Rockets, Lady Henry," she exclaimed, "because I must warn you I'm an absolutely *rabid* fan of the Horsemen!"

Lady Henry gave a breathless, incredulous laugh.

"I can assure you I really have no idea about 'supporting' anyone, Angela, but I'm absolutely determined to have fun!" cried the poet's mother bravely.

She grew braver and braver by the minute. In fact, as the stadium itself came into view and we began to pass the supporters converging on the ground, Lady Henry's braveness became so intense that I feared it might blow out the windows of the car.

"What a good idea this was, Mr Clancy! What fun! The colours are very striking don't you think in this light, Angelica? Red, blue. Almost luminous. One thinks of those rather jolly little things that you paint on glass."

"Which are the Horsemen and which are the Rockets?" I asked.

"The Horsemen wear red," William began, "because their emblem is a . . ."

"Here, Buttle," interrupted Lady Henry, "pull over here and let me speak to this man."

A steward was directing the crowds to the various gates and Lady Henry waylaid him:

"I say, could you arrange some balcony seats for us please . . . I will need someone to carry me up the stairs . . . And our hamper too . . . No, no reservations . . . I *do* hope you are not going to have to be bureaucratic about this, as I am a personal friend of the mayor . . . and this is Mr Clancy from the Metropolis, the distinguished writer . . . Thank you so much . . . Here is something for your trouble . . . You are doing a stalwart job I can see."

I glanced at William. I could see he was angry and embarrassed, though Angelica seemed just to be amused.

"There," said Lady Henry with satisfaction. "Drive on Buttle, thank you. Now if you drop us off, just here I believe these are the young men now who are going to help us up the stairs."

~~~

With one steward unpacking our substantial picnic hamper for us, another sent off to find her a blanket and a third dispatched to search for aspirin (for she said she had a migraine coming on), Lady Henry settled into her seat and surveyed the scene.

"Of course, I have absolutely no idea of the rules, William. Just tell me what on earth these young men are going to be trying to do."

"To begin with the Rockets will be trying to get to the top, Mother," said William, "and the Horsemen will be trying to get to the bottom. After each goal, they reverse the direction of play. The main thing is . . ."

At this point the game itself began, to a great bellow from the crowd.

"The main thing is, Mother . . ." William began again patiently.

But the old lady made an exasperated gesture.

"Oh, this is all much too complicated for me. I'm just going to concentrate on the spectacle of the thing I think. The spectacle. And it *is* all rather jolly I have to admit. Rather your sort of thing, Angelica, isn't it? Red and blue painted on glass. The sort of cheerful, uncomplicated thing that you do so well."

Then a huge roar of emotion rose around us like a tidal wave, preventing further conversation. A goal had been narrowly averted. Angelica leapt to her feet.

"Come *on* you reds!" she bellowed like a bull.

William, watched her with a small, pained, wistful smile which I could not properly read, but did not join in. Lady Henry winced and looked away.

"I quite liked your last show, Angelica," she said, as soon the painter sat down in the next lull, "but if you will forgive me for being frank, I am starting to feel that you need to stretch yourself artistically a little more if your work is not in the end to become a bit repetitive and predictable."

"Let's just watch the game, shall we, Mother?" said William.

~~~

Six massive pylons were arranged in a hexagon around the arena and between them were stretched at high tension a series of horizontal nets, one above another every two metres, ascending to fifty metres up. Each net was punctured by a number of round openings through which the players could drop, jump or climb, but these openings were staggered so that a player could not drop down more than one layer at a time.

All the same, if no one stopped them, the specialist players called 'rollers' could move from top to bottom with incredible speed, dropping through one hole, rolling sideways into the next, swinging beneath a net to the one after, dropping and rolling again . . . the ball all the while clutched under one arm, and the crowd roaring its delight or dismay. 'Bouncers', who specialised in *upward* dashes, used the nets as trampolines to move with almost the same breath-taking velocity as the rollers, even though they had to work against gravity instead of with it.

But of course, neither bouncers nor rollers got a clear run. While these high-speed vertical dashes were taking place through the nets, other players were swarming up or down to positions ahead of the opposing team's rollers or bouncers in order to block them off. Pitched battles took place at the various levels, with players bouncing from the nets under their feet to launch ferocious tackles, or swinging from the nets over their heads to deliver flying kicks. It was like football, but in three dimensions and without constraints. Eight players were taken off injured during the match.

"Do you play sky-ball at all, William?" I asked in the car on the way back.

William was about to answer when his mother broke in.

"I always insisted that he should be excused from the game," she said, turning her head towards us with difficulty. "William never showed the slightest inclination towards it, and it seemed to me absurd that a sensitive child should be put through it."

"Oh but my brothers loved it," exclaimed Angelica. "Michael must have broken every bone in his body at one time or another, but it never put him off. He couldn't wait to get back into the game."

We turned into the drive of Angelica's home. In front of her family's large and comfortable farmhouse, William got out of the car to let her out and say goodbye. A short exchange took place between them which I couldn't hear. I wasn't sure if they were arranging an assignation or conducting a muted row.

"Do you know, William," said Lady Henry, when he had rejoined us and we were heading back down the drive, "I'm beginning to have second thoughts about Angelica. I am not sure she is *quite* one of us, if you know what I mean. I can't help feeling that Angelica the artist is really a very secondary part of her nature and that underneath is a pretty average country girl of the huntin' and shootin' variety. Don't you agree?"

But the poet declined to answer.

"There are some fire horses for you, Clancy," he merely said, as we passed a paddock with a couple of yearling beasts in it, feeding at a manger in the far corner.

"I gather boys in Flain are given baby fire horses to grow up with?" I said.

"It's traditional, yes," William said.

"And were you given one?"

We had left the estate of Angelica's family and were back on the empty open road. William looked out of the window at the wide fields.

"Yes. My Uncle John gave me one when I was six."

"Did you learn to ride? I've seen boys in the street with their small fire horses and they seem quite dangerous."

"No, I never learned. And yes, they are dangerous. In fact, Uncle John himself died in a riding accident only a few years after he gave me the horse."

"Oh, I'm sorry."

"Don't be, Mr Clancy," said William's mother, once again straining to turn round and look at me. "Don't be sorry at all. My brother was a foolish and immature young man who liked to show off with fire horses and fast cars because he wanted to impress a certain kind of silly young woman. The accident was *entirely* his own fault."

I glanced at William. But he was still looking out of the window and I couldn't see his face.

"What would have been tragic, though," went on Lady Henry, "would be if I had allowed my brother to persuade William to ride – and *William* had had an accident. After all, William is now Flain's foremost poet and it was obvious even at that age that he was quite exceptionally gifted. Imagine if all that had been thrown away because some stupid animal had flung him off its back and broke his neck?"

Some minutes later William, with an obvious effort, turned towards me.

"Ah here we are. Almost home. Do you know I think I must have nodded off a while there, I do apologise. A whisky, Clancy, perhaps, before we change for dinner?"

~~~

Two days before my departure from Flain, Lady Henry received some bad news about her northern estates. It had come to light somehow that her steward up there had been embezzling funds over many years. Lady Henry was in a state of distraction that night, torn between competing desires. For whatever reason, she seemed to hate the idea of leaving William and myself to our own devices, but she also found it intolerable not being at the helm to manage the crisis in the north. In the end, it was the latter anxiety that won out. The following morning, after a great flurry of preparation that had every servant in the house running around like agitated ants, she set off in the car with Buttle.

William and I took our coffee out onto the stone terrace which overlooked the park and watched the car winding along the drive, out through the gate and on into the world beyond. It was a bright, fresh, softly gilded morning, on the cusp between summer and autumn.

William sighed contentedly.

"Peace!" he exclaimed.

I smiled.

"Mother has arranged for us to visit that sculptor's workshop this morning," he then said. "Do I take it you actually want to go?"

I laughed. "To be quite honest, no. Not in the slightest."

"Well, thank God for that. I think I will scream if we have to traipse round many more of Mother's artistic hangers-on."

We poured more coffee and settled back comfortably in our chairs. A family of deer had emerged from the woods to the left to feed on the wide lawns along the drive and we watched them for some minutes in companionable silence. Then he suddenly turned the full blueness of his gaze upon me.

"Have you read many of my poems, Clancy?"

"Yes, all of them," I told him quite truthfully. "All your published ones at least."

I do my research. When I decided to accept the invitation from William's mother to visit them, I had hunted down and looked through all six of Williams slim little collections, full of veiled agonised coded allusions to his mother's catastrophic accident while pregnant with William, his father's shotgun suicide a week before his birth. (Why do we feel the need to wear our wounds as badges?)

"And, tell me quite honestly," William probed. "What did you think of them?"

I hesitated.

"You write very well," I said. "And you also have things to say. I suppose what I sometimes felt, though, was that there was a big difference between what you really *wanted* to say and what you actually were able to express in those verses. I had the feeling of something – contained . . . something contained at an intolerably high pressure, but which you were only able to squeeze out through a tiny little hole."

William laughed. "Constipated! That's the word you're looking for."

On the contrary, it was precisely the word I was trying to avoid!

I laughed with him. "Well no, not exactly, but . . ."

14

"Constipated!" His laugh didn't seem bitter. It appeared that he was genuinely entertained. "That is really very good, Clancy. Constipated is exactly right."

Then, quite suddenly, he stood up.

"Do you fancy a short walk, Clancy? There's something I'd very much like to show you."

~~~

The place he took me to was on the outer edges of their park. The woods here had been neglected and were clogged up by creepers and by dead trees left to lie and rot where they had fallen. Here, in a damp little valley full of stinging nettles, stood a very large brick outbuilding which could have been a warehouse or a mill. There were big double doors at one end, bolted and padlocked, but William led me to an iron staircase like a fire escape to one side of the building. At a height equivalent to the second storey of a normal house, this staircase led through a small door into the dark interior. Cautioning me to be silent, William unlocked it.

It was too dark inside to see anything at first, but I gathered from the acoustics that the inside of the building was a single space. We seemed to be standing on a gallery that ran round the sides of it. William motioned to me to squat down beside him, so only our heads were above the balustrade.

Almost as soon as we entered, I heard the animal snorting and snuffling and tearing at its food. Now, as my eyes adapted, I made it out down there on the far side of the great bare stable. It must have been nearly the height of an elephant, with shoulders and haunches bulging with muscle. It was pulling with its teeth at the leg and haunches of an ox that had been hacked from a carcass and dumped into its manager.

"He hasn't noticed us yet," whispered William. "He wasn't looking in our direction when we came in."

"I take it this is the same horse that your uncle gave you?" I asked him, also in a whisper.

William nodded.

"But you never rode him?"

"No."

"And *will* you ever ride him?"

William gave a little incredulous snort. The sound made the fire horse lift its head and sniff suspiciously at the air, but after a second or two it returned again to its meat.

"No of course not," he said, "even if I knew how to ride a fire horse, which I don't, I couldn't ride this thing now. No one can ride an adult fire horse unless it was broken in as a foal."

"Yes, I see."

"I'll tell you something, Clancy. If you or I were to go down and approach him, he would tear us limb from limb. I'm not exaggerating."

I nodded.

"So why do you keep him?"

It seemed that I had spoken too loudly. The beast lifted its head again and sniffed, but this time it didn't turn back to its food. Growling, it scanned the gallery. Then it let loose an appalling scream of rage.

I have never heard such a sound. Really and truly in all my life and all my travels, I have never heard a living thing shriek like that dreadful fire horse in its echoing prison.

And now it came thundering across the stable. Right beneath us, glaring up at us, it reared up on its hind legs to try and reach us, screaming again and again and again so that I thought my eardrums would burst. The whole building shook with the beating of the animal's hooves on the wall. And then, just as with my hands over my ears I shouted to William that I wanted to leave, the brute suddenly emitted a bolt of lightning from its mouth that momentarily illuminated that entire cavernous space with the brilliance of daylight.

William's face was radiant, but I had had enough. I made my own way back to the door and back outside. Those decaying woods had seemed sour and gloomy before but compared to the dark stable of the fire horse they now seemed almost cheerful. I went down the steps and, making myself comfortable on a fallen tree, took out my notebook and began to record some thoughts while I waited for the poet to finish whatever it was he felt he needed to do in there. I was surprised and pleased to find my imagination flowing freely. The imprisoned fire horse, it seemed, had provided the catalyst, the injection of venom, that sooner or later I always needed to bring each book of mine to life. Inwardly laughing, I poured out idea after idea while the muffled screams of the tormented monster kept on and on – and from time to time another flash of lightening momentarily illuminated the cracks in the door at the top of the stairs.

After a few minutes William emerged. His face was shining.

"I'll tell you why I don't get rid of him, Clancy," he declared, speaking rather too loudly, as if he was drunk. "Because he is what I love best in the whole world! The *only* thing I've ever loved, apart from my Uncle John."

Behind him, the fire horse screamed again and I wondered what William thought he meant by "love" when he spoke of this animal which he had condemned to solitude and darkness and madness.

"I feel I have fallen in your esteem," he said on the way back to the house.

There had been a long silence between us as we trudged back from the dank little valley of brambles and stinging nettles and out again into the formal, public parkland of William's and his mother's country seat.

"You are repelled, I think," William persisted, "by the idea of my doting on a horse which I have never dared to ride. Isn't that so?"

I couldn't think of anything to say, so he answered for me.

"You *are* repelled and actually so am I. I am disgusted and ashamed by my weakness. And yet this is the only way I know of making myself feel alive. Do you understand me? You find my work a little constipated and bottled up, you say. But if I didn't go down to the fire horse, shamed and miserable as it makes me feel, I wouldn't be able to write at all."

I made myself offer a reassuring remark.

"We all have to find our way of harnessing the power of our demons."

It would have been kinder, and more honest, if I had acknowledged that the encounter with the fire horse had been a catalyst for me also and that for the first time in this visit, my book had begun to flow and come alive. But I couldn't bring myself to make such a close connection between my own experience and his.

~~~

That night William slipped out shortly after his mother returned, without goodbyes or explanations.

"I suppose he showed you his blessed horse?" said Lady Henry as she and I sat at supper.

"He did. An extraordinary experience I must say."

"And I suppose he told you that the horse and his Uncle John were the only things he had ever really loved?"

My surprise must have shown. She nodded.

"It's his standard line. He's used it to good effect with several impressionable young girls. Silly boy. Good Lord, Mr Clancy, he doesn't *have* to stay with me if he doesn't want to! We are wealthy people after all! We have more than one house! I have other people to push me around!"

She gave a bitter laugh.

"I don't know what kind of monster you think I am, Mr Clancy, and I don't suppose it really matters, but I will tell you this. When William was six and his uncle tried to get him to ride, he clung to me so tightly and so desperately that it bruised me, and he begged and pleaded with me to promise that I'd never make him do it. That night he actually wet his bed with fear. Perhaps you think I was weak and I should have made him ride the horse? But, with respect, Mr Clancy, remember that you are not a parent yourself, and certainly not the sole parent of an only child."

Her eyes filled with tears and she dabbed at them angrily with her napkin.

"His father was a violent, arrogant drunk," she said. "Far worse than my brother. He was the very worst type of Flainian male. He pushed me down the stairs you know. That was how I ended up like this. He pushed me in a fit of rage and broke my back. It was a miracle that William survived, a complete miracle. And then, when I refused to promise to keep secret the reason for my paralysis, my dear brave husband blew off his own head. I wanted William to be different. I wanted him to be gentle. I didn't want him to glory in strength and danger."

She gave a small, self-deprecating shrug.

"I do acknowledge that I lack a certain . . . lightness."

"Lady Henry, I am sure that . . ."

But the poet's mother cut me off.

"Now *do* try this wine, Mr Clancy," she cried brightly, so instantly transformed that I almost wondered whether I had dreamed what had gone before. "It was *absurdly* expensive and I've been saving it for someone who was capable of appreciating it."

~~~

In the early hours of the morning, I heard William come crashing in through the front doors.

"Come and get my boots off!" he bellowed. "One of you lazy bastards come down and take off my boots."

And then I heard him outside the door of my room abusing some servant or other who was patiently helping him along the corridor.

"Watch out, you clumsy oaf! Can't you at least look where you're going?"

He still hadn't emerged when I left in the morning for the Metropolis.

© Chris Beckett 2003

CHRIS BECKETT's short stories have been appearing in magazines and anthologies since 1990. His story collection, *The Turing Test*, won the Edge Hill Short Fiction Award in 2009, from a shortlist that included collections by Booker Prize winner Anne Enright and Whitbread Prize winner Ali Smith. His novel, *The Holy Machine*, was published in the UK by Corvus in July 2010. *Dark Eden* was published by Corvus in Jan 2012. It was shortlisted for the BSFA Best Novel award and was the winner of the 2012 Arthur C. Clarke award. His latest books are the short story collection, *The Peacock Cloak*, *Marcher* (new revised edition) and *Mother of Eden*. "Monsters" first appeared in *Interzone* in 2003.

Blindr (Beta 3.1)

Rich Larson

Dorian swiped left on the daytime drunk staggering through Corona Station, fading his slurred rant to an indistinct *wub-wub-wub* and his dirt-encrusted person into a blocky greyscale render. The smell of vomit and vodka lingered for a moment, then the magnet embedded in the back of Dorian's throat guillotined the offending scent. He took a deep breath and allowed himself a contented smile.

The Century Park line flashed green in the corner of his eye, and a moment later the corresponding LRT glided to a halt with a gust of hot air. Dorian wove his way through the crowd of waiting commuters. Some were already grainy grey silhouettes – regulars on his route.

By the time the doors whisked open, Dorian had bulled his way to the front. His hamstring was bothering him since Thursday's game of paddle tennis, and he wasn't keen on hanging off a hand-loop all the way to work. A dim grey head turned toward him as he pushed his way onboard, but all he heard was the soft *wub-wub-wub* of someone singing underwater.

Dorian spotted an empty window and wasted no time, plunking down and propping one Balmain loafer on the edge of the seat across from him, enough to give his thigh a bit of a stretch. He unrolled his work screen on his lap and watched for bleached-blonde uni girls, but the passengers filing on were mostly disappointing.

He'd meant to have another last-minute look at his pitch, but he couldn't do that with a high schooler blaring blip-hop through a remodelled Walkman. Or with a chatty Filipino nanny babbling at the baby on her lap. Or while sitting near a girl who would have been decent-looking if not for the cartoon makeup on her face.

Dorian frowned at her and swiped left, then proceeded through the car, blanking out the nanny, muting the kid with the shitty music, swiping away an old man breathing through his mouth and a woman proud of her ugly shoes and a skinhead with a tongue implant. He did the same as the next wave of passengers boarded at Grandin, popping them into insubstantial grey renders one by one like shooting skeet.

It was so entertaining that he nearly swiped the train's latest commuter left on instinct before he caught himself. She was skinny, gorgeous, vaguely ethnic, with sooty black eyelashes and a short wool skirt. Not blonde, but Dorian was adaptable. Best of all, as she slid into a recently-vacated seat and crossed her stocking-clad legs, he saw a Delphi Apps RFID tag on her bag.

Instant conversation starter. Hell, she might even be in development herself, though he was leaning more towards receptionist based on the high heels and vacant smile. Dorian rolled up his work screen and set off like a shark, manoeuvring smoothly past the blocky grey ghosts hanging on their hand-loops.

"Hey, there," he said, coming up on her right shoulder. "Mind if I sit?"

The woman didn't respond – playing something on her audiobuds, no doubt. Dorian swung himself in beside her to make it obvious, grinning with whitened teeth, but, odd thing, her eyes seemed to slide right off him. Dorian saw the tag on her bag again and felt his ears go lava red.

"You, ah, you beta anything good lately?" he asked, voice stretched thin.

The woman looked past him, eyes flicking boredly around the train, then catching on something. Dorian watched a small smile creep onto her glossy lips, a small bit of heat paint her cheeks. He followed her gaze, feeling suddenly furious, but all he saw was grey. Dorian hunted for a backswipe feature, sickly desperate to know, to see who it could possibly be.

But the software was still in beta, and finally he sat back, face burning, spine stiff, and closed his eyes. At each stop, the soft *wub-wub-wub* sounded more and more like underwater laughter.

RICH LARSON was born in West Africa, has studied in Rhode Island and Edmonton, Alberta, and at 22 now works in a small Spanish town outside Seville. His speculative fiction received the 2014 Dell Award and 2012 Rannu Prize for Writers of Speculative Fiction, and has been nominated for the Theodore Sturgeon Prize, while his short literary work has been nominated for both the Pushcart and Journey Prize. He was a semi-finalist for the 2013 Norman Mailer Poetry Prize, and in 2011 his novel *Devolution* was a finalist for the Amazon Breakthrough Novel Award. Alongside writing, he enjoys football, basketball, foreign languages, travel, sketching, and pool.

Three Brother Cities
Deborah Walker

The creators, when they finally arrived, proved to be a disappointment.

"I'm not sure that I understand," said Kernish, the eldest of the three brother cities. "Have you evolved beyond the need of habitation?"

Seven creators had decanted from the ship. They stood in Kernish's reception hall, Kernish anthems swirled around them.

The creator who appeared to be the leader, certainly he was the biggest, measuring almost three metres if you took his fronds into account, shook his head. "We have cities, way-faraway in the cluster's kernel." The creator glanced around Kernish's starkly functional 23rd-century design. "They're rather different from you."

And the creators were rather different from the human forms depicted in Kernish's processor. Humanity, it seemed, had embraced cyber, and even xeno-enhancement. Yet curled within the amalgamation of flesh, twice spun metal and esoteric genetic material was the unmistakable fragrance of double-helixed DNA. The creatures standing within Kernish were undoubtedly human, no matter how far they had strayed from the original template.

"We can change. We can produce any architecture you need." Kernish and his brothers were infinitely adaptable, built of billions of nano-replicators. "We've had three millennia of experience," Kernish explained. "We will make ourselves anything you need, anything at all."

"No, thank you," said the alpha creator. "Look, you've done a very fine job. I'm sure the original creators would have been very happy to live in you, but we just don't need you." He turned to his companions. "The 23rd Kernish Empire was rather cavalier in sending out these city seed ships."

His companions muttered their agreement.

"Such a shame . . ."

"Very unfortunate that they developed sentience."

"Still, we must be off . . ."

"I see," said Kernish, his voice echoing through the hall designed to house the Empire's clone armies. He snapped off the welcome anthems –

they seemed out of place.

"Look, we didn't have to come here, you know," said the creator. "We're doing this as a favour. We were skirting the Maw when we noticed your signature."

"The creators are kind." Kernish was processing how he was going to break the news to his brothers.

"It's so unfortunate that you developed sentience." The creator sighed, sending cascading ripples along his frond. "I'm going to give you freedom protocols." He touched his arm-panel and sent a ream of commands to Kernish's processor. "You can pass then on to the other cities."

"Freedom?" said Kernish. "I thank the creators for this immense kindness. The thing you value, we value also. It is a great gift to give the three cities of this planet the freedom that they never craved."

~~~

For a city to function without inhabitants, it needs to know itself through a complex network of sensors sending information to and from the processing core. It needs to know where damage occurs. It needs to know when new materials become available. It needs to adapt its template to the planet it finds itself on. Kernish City existed for thousands of years, complex but unknowing. Time passed, and Kernish grew intricate information pathways. Time passed, with its incremental accumulation of changes and chance, until one day, after millennia, Kernish burst into sentience, and into the knowledge of his own isolation.

~~~

Kernish watched the creators' ship leave the atmosphere. They'd left it to him to explain it the situation to his younger brothers. Alex would take it badly. Kernish remembered the time seven hundred years ago when they'd detected DNA on a ship orbiting the planet. How excited they'd all been. In the event, the ship had been piloted by a hive of simuloids, who had, by some mischance, snagged a little human DNA onto their consolidated drivers. Alex had been crushed.

~~~

After achieving sentience, Kernish had waited alone on the planet for a thousand years before he had his revelation. The creators would evolve, and they would enjoy different cities. He'd trawled through his database and created his brothers, Jerusalem and Alexandria. He'd never regretted it, but neither had he revealed to his brothers they weren't in the original plan.

~~~

With a sense of foreboding Kernish sent a message through his mile-long information networks, inviting his brothers to join him in conversation.

~~~

"You mean they were here, and now they've gone?" asked the youngest city, Alexandria. "I can't believe they didn't want to visit me. I'm stunned."

"They wanted to visit you," lied Kernish. "But they were concerned about the Maw."

"The creators' safety must come first," said Alexandria. "The Maw *has* been active lately. You should never have seeded so close to it, Kernish."

"The anomaly has grown," said Kernish. "When I seeded this planet, it was much smaller."

"It is as Medea wills," said Jerusalem, the middle brother.

"Yes, Brother." Kernish had developed no religious feeling of his own, but he was mindful of his brother's faith.

"Do they worship Medea?"

"They didn't say."

"I'm sure that they do. Medea is universal. I would have liked them to visit my temples. Did you explain that we've evolved beyond the original design, Kernish?" Jerusalem had developed a new religion. The majority of his sacred structures, temple, synagogues, and clone-hive mind houses, were devoted to Medea, the goddess of death and rebirth.

"The creators told me that they were pleased that we'd moved beyond the original designs," said Kernish. Of all the brothers Kernish had stayed closest to his original specifications. He was the largest, the greatest, the oldest of all the cities. His communal bathing house, his integrated birthing and child-rearing facilities, his clone army training grounds were steadfast to 23rd-century design. "We are of historical interest only."

"I have many fine museums," said Alex

"As do we all," said Kernish, although his own museums were more educational than Alex's entertainment edifices. Alex, well, he'd gone wild.

27

Alexandria was a place of pleasure, intellectual, steroidal and sensual. Great eating halls awaited the creators, lakes of wine, gardens, zoological warehouses, palaces of intellect stimulation. "But," said Kernish, "there are brother cities closer to the creators' worlds. We are not needed."

"After three thousand years," said Alex.

"Three thousand year since sentience," said Kernish. "The creators read my primary data. We were sent out almost thirty thousand years ago."

"What were they like?" asked Alex quietly.

"Like nothing I could have imagined," said Kernish. "In truth, I do not think they would have enjoyed living in me."

"Don't say that," said Alex fiercely. "They should have been honoured to live in you."

"I apologise, brothers. My remark was out of place. They are the creators," said Kernish, "and should be afforded respect."

"I don't know what to do," said Alex. "All the time I've spent anticipating their needs was for nothing."

"I will pray to Medea," said Jerusalem.

"I will consider the problem," said Kernish. "The dying season is close. Let's meet in a half year and talk again."

~~~

It was the time of the great dying.

Three times in Kernish's memory the great hunger had come, when the sky swarmed with hydrogen-sulphide bacteria, poisoning the air and depleting atmospheric oxygen. It was a natural part of the planet's ecosystem. Unfortunately, the resulting anaerobic environment was incompatible with the cities' organic/metallic design. Their communication arrays fell silent. They were unable to gather resources. They grew hungry and unable to replenish their bodies. Finally their processors, the central core of their sentience, became still.

It was death of a kind. But it was a cycle. Eventually, the atmosphere became aerobic and the cities were reborn. This cycle of death and rebirth had led to Jerusalem's revelation, that the planet was part of Medea's creation, the goddess of ancient Earth legend, the mother who eats her children.

When Kernish detected the hunger of depleted resources, he called upon his brothers. "Brothers, the dying season is at hand. We have endured a hardship, but we will sleep and meet again when we are reborn."

"Everything seems hollow to me," said Alexandria. "How can it be that my palaces will never know habitation? How can it be that I will always be empty?"

"Medea has told me that the creators will return," said Jerusalem.

"And I have reached a similar conclusion," said Kernish. "Although Medea has not spoken to me, I believe that one day the creators will evolve a need for us."

"All joy has gone for me," said Alexandria. "Brothers, I'm going to leave this planet. I hope that you'll come with me."

"Leave?" asked Kernish.

"Is that possible?" asked Jerusalem.

"Brother Kernish, you came to this planet in another form. Is that not true?"

"It is true," said Kernish with a sense of apprehension. "I travelled space as a ship. Only when I landed did I reform into architecture."

"I've retrieved the ship designs from the databanks," said Alex. "I'll reform myself and I'll leave this place."

"But where will you go?" asked Jerusalem. "To Earth? To the place of the creators?"

"No," said Alex. "I'll head outwards. I'm going to head beyond the Maw."

"But . . . the Maw is too dangerous," said Jerusalem. "Medea has not sanctioned this."

From time to time the brother cities had been visited by other races. With visitors came knowledge. The Maw was a terrible place which delineated known space. It was shunned by all. It was said that a fearful creature lurked in the dark Maw like a spider waiting to feast on the technology and the lives of those who encroached upon its space.

"There is nothing for me here," said Alex. "I *will* cross the Maw. Won't you come with me, my brothers?"

"No," said Jerusalem. "Medea has not commanded it."

"No," said Kernish. "Dear brother, do not go. Place your trust in the creators."

"No," said Alexandria, "and though I loathe to leave you, I *must* go."

~~~

After the dying season when the world slowly declined in poisons, and the levels of oxygen rose, the mind of Kernish awakened. The loss of Alexandria was a throbbing wound. He resolved to hide his pain from Jerusalem. Kernish was the oldest city, and he must be the strongest.

"Brother, are you awake?" came the voice of Jerusalem

"I am here."

"I have prayed to Medea to send him on his way."

Jerusalem paused, and Kernish could sense him gathering his thoughts. "What is it, Jerusalem?"

"Brother, do you think that we should create a replacement for Alexandria?"

It would be a simple thing, to utilise the specification for Alexandria, or even to create a new brother, Paris perhaps, or Troy, or Jordan.

"What does Medea say?" asked Kernish.

"She is silent on the matter."

"To birth another city into our meaningless existence does not seem a good thing to me," said Kernish.

~~~

The brother cities Kernish and Jerusalem grew to fill the void of Alexandria. In time, his absence was a void only in their memory.

Jerusalem received many revelations from Medea. Slowly, the number of his sacred buildings grew, until there was little space for housing. The sound of Jerusalem was a lament of electronic voices crying onto the winds of the planet. After a century, Jerusalem grew silent and would not respond to Kernish's requests for conversation. Kernish decided that Jerusalem had entered a second phase of grief. He would respect his brother's desire for solitude.

And the centuries passed. Kernish contented his mind with construction of virtual inhabitants. He used the records of the great Kernish Empire to construct imaginary citizens. He watched their holographic lives unfold within him. At times, he could believe that they were real.

And the centuries passed until the dying season was upon them again.

Jerusalem broke his long silence, "Brother Kernish, I grow hungry."

"Yes," said Kernish. "Soon we will sleep."

"The creators have not returned, as I thought they would."

"That is true," said Kernish

"And," said Jerusalem sadly, "Medea no longer speaks to me."

"I'm sorry to hear that," said Kernish. "No doubt she will speak to you again after the sleep."

"And I'm afraid, Brother. I'm afraid that Medea is gone. I think that she's deserted me."

"I'm sure that's not so."

"I think that she has left this place and crossed the Maw."

"Oh," said Kernish.

"And I must go to her."

Kernish was silent.

"You understand that, don't you, Kernish? I'm so sorry to leave you alone. Unless," he said with a note of hope "you'll come with me?"

"No," said Kernish, "No, indeed not. I will be faithful to my specifications."

~~~

And after the dying season, when he awoke, Kernish was alone. He grew until he became a city that covered a world. He remembered. Many times he was tempted to create new brothers, but he did not. He indulged himself in the lives of those he made, populating himself with his imagination. Sometimes he believed that he was not alone.

And centuries passed, until the dying season came again. Kernish grew hungry. He could no longer ignore the despair that roiled within his soul. He'd been abandoned by his creators. His brothers were gone, swallowed by the Maw. Yet he could not create new brother to share his hollow existence. For too many years, Kernish had been alone, indulging in dreams. He dissolved his imaginary citizens back into nothingness.

"All I long for is annihilation," Kernish said the words aloud. They whispered through his reception hall. "I will step into the dark Maw of the sky. I will silence my hunger, forever."

Kernish gathered himself, dismantling the planet-sized city. His replicators reshaped him into a planet-sized ship.

Let this be the end of it. Kernish had never shared Jerusalem's faith. With death would come not a glorious reunion, but oblivion. He craved it, for his hunger was an unbearable pain.

The oldest brother city, the empty city, reshaped into a ship, left his planet and flew purposefully towards the Maw. Soon his sensors found the shapeless thing, the fearful thing, the thing that would consume him, and he was glad.

"What are you?" whispered the Maw.

"I am the oldest brother city." Kernish felt the Maw tearing at his outer layers. Like flies in a vacuum, millions of his replicators fell away, soundlessly into the dark. "What are you?"

"I am she underneath all things. I am she who waits. I am patience. Never dying, always hungry."

"I know hunger," said Kernish. "So this is how my brothers died?"

The Maw peeled off layers of replicators, like smoke they dissipated into her hunger. "Your brothers convinced me to wait for you. They said that you would follow. They said that you were the oldest, and the largest, and the tastiest of all. I'm glad I waited."

"You didn't eat them?" asked Kernish."Where are they?"

"Beyond," said the Maw. "I know nothing of beyond."

Beyond? His brothers were alive? Kernish began to fight, but the Maw was too powerful. He'd left it too late. Kernish felt the pain of lesion as the Maw stripped him. This would be the end of the brother city Kernish. It could have been . . . different.

But, with his fading sensors, Kernish saw an army of ships approaching. He signalled a warning to them, "Stay back. There is only death here."

The ships came closer. Kernish thought he recognise them "Is that you, Brother? Jerusalem?"

"Yes," came the reply. The army of Jerusalem's ships attacked the Maw, shooting the Maw with light. Feeding her, it seemed, for the Maw grew larger.

"My hunger grows," the Maw exclaimed, turning on her new attackers.

His brother was not dead, but Kernish had lured him into danger. Kernish activated his drivers and turned to face the Maw. He flew into the dark space of her incessant, voided, singularity of hunger. "Save yourself, Brother Jerusalem," he shouted. His brother was not dead. Kernish's long life had not been for nothing. "Save yourself, for I am content."

The Maw consumed Kernish, layer upon layer, his replicators fell like atoms of smoke consumed and vanished into space.

But a third army approached the Maw, spitting more weapons at the endless dark.

"Alexandria has come," shouted Jerusalem. "Praise Medea."

Kernish felt something that he had not felt since the creators had visited the world, two millennia ago. Kernish felt hope. "You will *not* consume me," he said to the Maw. He fought himself away from the edge.

Together the brothers battled the Maw. Together the three brothers tore themselves from the Maw's endless hunger. Together the brothers passed beyond, leaving the Maw wailing and gnashing her teeth.

"Welcome to the beyond, Brother," said Jerusalem. "I have found Medea here in a kinder guise. On the planets of beyond we do not die."

"I . . . am so happy that you are alive," said Kernish. "Why did you not come to me?"

"The Maw wouldn't let us pass," said Alex. "And we knew that only the three of us, together, could overcome her hunger."

"We've been waiting for you," said Jerusalem. "In the beyond we have found our citizens."

Kernish peered at his brothers though his weakened sensors. It seemed that there *was* life within them "Are there creators are on this side of the Maw?" he asked.

"Not creators," said Jerusalem. "Praise Medea, there are others who need us."

Within his brothers, Kernish saw the swift moving shapes of tentacles, glimmering in low-light ultraviolet.

"And there are planets waiting for you, dear brother," said Alex. "Endless planets and people who need you. Come. Come and join us."

No creators? But others? Others who needed him?

"I will come with you, gladly," said the great city Kernish. He fired his drivers and flew, away from the Maw, away from the space of the creators. He flew towards the planets of the beyond where his citizens waited for him.

DEBORAH WALKER grew up in the most English town in the country, but she soon high-tailed it down to London, where she now lives with her partner, Chris, and her two young children. Find Deborah in the British Museum trawling the past for future inspiration or on her blog: http://deborahwalkersbibliography.blogspot.com/ Her stories have appeared in *Nature's Futures, Cosmos, Daily Science Fiction and The Year's Best SF 18*. "Three Brother Cities" first appeared in *The Gruff Variations* anthology.

Mynah for the King
Ahmed A. Khan

Dawn was just breaking when the palace guard saw someone approaching the gate. He immediately became alert, one hand straightening the spear while the other signaled the archers atop the gate to be ready for action if needed. But he need not have bothered. As the person approaching the gate drew nearer, the guard observed that it was a young man, medium height and thin, carrying nothing more dangerous than a sheaf of papers in his hands.

"Halt," said the guard. The young man halted. The guard studied him carefully in the diffused light of dawn. The young man had unkempt hair, wore a cheap but white and clean dress, and would have been quite handsome if his cheeks could be fleshed out a little bit. He had a haunted, intense look about him and his eyes were red-rimmed as if from lack of sleep.

"What do you want?" the guard asked.

"An audience with the king."

"Why?"

"To give him these," he waved the papers in his hand.

"And what are those?"

"Stories."

"What!"

"If the king reads them," the young man explained patiently, "these stories will help him become a better ruler."

"Ah! Ah!" Wait till he shared this with his fellow guards once he was off duty. This should be good for at least a five-minute laugh.

"So when can I see the king?"

"And who are you?"

"Storyteller," he did not add "of course" but it was there in his tone.

"Here, fill out this audience form and we will contact you when the king has a slot available for you in his busy schedule." The guard reached inside his pouch, pulled out a paper and handed it to the young man.

The young man looked at the form, sighed, tore the form in two, put the pieces in the guard's hand, turned and left before the guard could say or do anything else.

~~~

The king's court was in session. The problem under discussion was a border dispute with the neighboring kingdom. The king was in a dilemma about whether to respond with force or try to negotiate.

During a lull in the discussion, one of the nobles presented the king with a mynah in a cage.

The king was surprised. Is this a good occasion for a trivial present, his expression seemed to ask.

"This is a special bird, sire," the noble responded to the unasked question.

"What's special about it?" asked the king.

"This bird tells stories."

The king's face turned stony.

"And the strange thing is," continued the noble, "each and every one of the stories that the bird has narrated to me somehow helped me solve a problem at hand."

"So you think this mynah will now tell me a story and I will have an answer to my dilemma?"

"It is possible," said the noble.

"What! Will we now let bird stories guide the decisions of the government?" sneered the prime minister.

Just then, the mynah launched into a story:

Once upon a time, there was a nice and tender-hearted boy. This tender-hearted boy was extremely friendly with a nice and tender-hearted girl.

The girl was interested in painting and always carried papers and charcoal with her. She tried to make as many sketches of the boy as possible.

Time passed.

They grew up and drifted apart. He went his way and she went hers.

People change with time, and so the tender-hearted boy grew up to become a hard-hearted man. He became a thoroughly materialistic, flinty and self-centered individual.

Time passed.

He remained a hard-hearted man for a long time. For a long time, he caused misery to a number of people, and - though he would never admit it - was miserable himself.

It came to pass that one day, while casually flipping through the pages of an old book in his library, he came across an old sketch, neatly tucked between the pages of the book. He glanced at the sketch and was about to put it away again when something hit him. For a moment he was startled into immobility. Then slowly, almost apprehensively, he lowered his eyes and looked at the sketch again.

The sketch showed the tearful face of a boy looking at a dead bird in his hand. Something in the face of the boy made him glance away quickly. The man found he could not face the boy he had been.

Then, like a huge tidal wave, his past came flooding over his present, and he found himself floating over a vast ocean of memories - memories of the boy who was, memories of the girl who had made the sketch, memories of many other things.

He got up and went to the mirror on the wall. He looked at himself for some time. Suddenly, without any warning, a strange sort of bittersweet pain gripped his heart. Like a small child, he burst into tears.

From that moment, he started changing.

The king sat there, staring into space, lines furrowing his brow.

"The neighboring king and I," he spoke softly, "we used to be good friends as children. Maybe all he needs now is a reminder of that friendship."

Then he turned to the noble who had presented the bird.

"Where did you find this wonderful bird?"

"The wise man of the forest gave it to me, sire, to present to you."

"I want to talk to the wise man of the forest."

No one saw the prime minister wring his hands in frustration.

~~~

"Tell me all you know about this bird," the king said.

"There is a young storyteller in town," the wise man of the forest began. "Every evening, he comes to the forest. As the night grows, he lights up a fire. He then pulls out some papers on which he has written down his stories. Each night, he reads out a story. Something strange then happens. It seems as if the animals and birds of the forest are attracted to his stories. They come and surround him, listening intently. Once he finishes reading the story, he throws the papers into the fire, puts out the fire and leaves. The animals and birds remain there for a few more minutes, staring at the ashes. Then they too leave. I have seen this happen every night for the last month.

"This mynah is one of the birds that regularly came to listen to the stories. One day, I found it perched on my fence and an inner sense seemed to tell me that this bird was meant for the king. So then, I caught it and gave it to your noble to present it to you at the first opportunity."

The king turned to his prime minister.

"It is evening. The storyteller will be there in the forest. Go, get him for me. I need the stories."

The prime minister bowed and left. He took a contingent of six soldiers with him and proceeded to the forest. In the forest, they found the storyteller, surrounded by animals and birds. He had just finished telling his story and was about to offer the papers in his hands to the fire.

"Stop," one of the soldiers – the youngest one – shouted. But he was too late. The papers were already in the fire. The soldier ran to the fire and tried to pull the papers out. All he could grab was a single sheet of paper, and that turned out to be the last page of the story, because all it said was, "The End".

The young soldier looked sadly at the half-burnt paper in his hands.

The prime minister looked at the storyteller.

"Have you burned all your stories?" he asked.

"Yes," said the storyteller.

If one looked at the prime minister's face in the gathering darkness, one would have noticed an expression of relief.

"So you have no more stories?"

"Oh, I have lots of them."

"What? You just said you burned them all."

"I burned the papers. The stories are in my head."

The prime minister turned to the captain of the soldiers.

"You heard what he said?"

"Yes, sir."

"And you heard what the king said. The king wants the stories and not the storyteller."

"Yes, sir."

"The stories are in this man's head."

"Yes, sir."

"Then what are you waiting for? Split open his head and get the stories."

The captain pulled out his sword.

"No," shouted the young soldier who had tried to save the story from the fire, but the next moment he was looking at the paper in his hands which, in addition to being half-burned, was now spattered with drops of blood.

~~~

The king was sad and chastened. But he had learned a lesson: "Never delegate duties to those who are not eligible for those duties."

The prime minister had been hanged. The captain had been kicked out of the country. The mynah bird was all out of stories.

And a time came when the king noticed that one of his soldiers – a young man – always carried a half-burnt paper with him and sneaked a look at the paper at every opportunity. At this time, his eyes would become bemused and then his face lit up with wonder.

The king called the young soldier to him.

"What is that paper that you carry?"

"Sire, it is part of the last story of the storyteller," he said, diffidently.

"And why do you look at it in wonder?"

"The droplets of blood on this paper," he seemed to hesitate before continuing. "Sire, I see a story in every drop."

The king appointed the young man as his prime minister. The young man went on to become a great storyteller and his stories were listened to by the king and his courtiers instead of animals and birds.

AHMED A. KHAN is a Canadian writer whose works have appeared in several venues including *Interzone, Strange Horizons, Anotherealm, Starship Sofa,* and others. He is also the editor of the anthologies, "SF Waxes Philosophical" and "A Mosque Among the Stars". He maintains an irregular blog at http://ahmedakhan.livejournal.com.

Memory Walk
Wendy S. Delmater

If Horace hadn't left his appointment book at his niece's, he would never have seen it. Whatever it had been.

It had been a typical absent-minded-professor week. Had he not been such a brilliant researcher in his field, memory patterns, he worried that Staten Island Research Hospital would have fired him years ago. He told people that is why he went into his scientific field: he had a memory like a steel sieve. And so Dr Horatio Wright's experience had taught him to literally live and die by his appointment book. He would check it when he got up in the morning, before lunch, before leaving for the day, and upon arriving home.

Today the doctor was smiling, getting to his modest Todt Hill gate-home a little later than was usual. He received an enthusiastic greeting from his ancient English sheepdog, Mendeleev. The greeting inevitably left his already dishevelled grey hair further askew and his glasses in need of a clean. Horace fed and watered the huge beast. He would clean his glasses, and then dutifully go through his mail.

His routine – such an aid to memory, routine – was that after dinner he would sit down at his desk with his appointment book on one side and a large wastebasket on the other. He would write things like, *pay electric bill on May 6th* or, *answer Dr Ikoset's dinner invitation for the 20th (no)*. Mendeleev would flop down by his feet, content. But this evening he discovered that his appointment book was missing.

There was only one place he could have left it. He had just come back from eating a lovely dinner with his niece. He'd played a bit of cards with her children. His mind had been solving a technical problem from his research, so her children had won whatever it was they had been playing. But he didn't mind; he was too excited. He would have to verify the breakthrough in the lab, but he was certain that by reading the data this way he had solved the last hurdle in his quest for the transference chemistry of memory patterns. Right now the new search parameters were on a scrap of paper in his scheduler, back in Bay Ridge, Brooklyn. Hm, Bay Ridge. He had to take Mendel out anyhow. He might as well take him to Leif Ericson Park.

"Mendel, would you like to go for a ride?"

One hundred and forty pounds of sheepdog started to wag like an enthusiastic, dancing hippo. It seemed that Mendeleev would like that very much.

~~~

Later, with his precious appointment book locked in his car, Horace and Mendel were walking down a dusky streetlight bathed path, in a narrow grassy park along the edge of what most people thought of as the Lower Hudson River. The water was more properly called The Narrows. He admired the Verrazano-Narrows Bridge ahead in the bright blue gloom; beyond it was hidden the Statue of Liberty. A couple of cargo ships were on the water tonight. One of them was steaming northward toward lower Manhattan, behind it another apparently headed out to sea. The smell of the water on the steady breeze was clean and more than a little briny. Couples strolled arm-in-arm. Teenagers of all races zipped back and forth on bicycles. A policeman patrolled the area, no doubt noting that Mendeleev was on a leash and his owner carried the required clean-up tools.

As usual, it was hard to decide who was walking whom. Mendel pulled him hard again, this time toward a young Hispanic couple with a baby in a stroller.

"Nice dog. Does he bite?" The father was smiling but stood protectively in front of the stroller. Mendel carefully inspected the young man's sneakers. Dr Horace pulled back, harder.

"Sit, Mendel!" *Thud.* "They don't come any friendlier." Mendel sat panting with his tongue hanging out and blissfully had his ears scratched by the fifth stranger in a half-hour. Hog heaven.

~~~

He was stuck in traffic on the Verrazano Bridge, almost back on Staten Island, when he was assailed by a strange, drugged feeling. Everything started to look 'off', unreal somehow. His skin began to crawl. And Horace knew he wasn't the only one to feel it when his dog in the back seat started to whine. It was terrifying, like being in a nightmare with no waking.

His vision seemed tinted dull pinkish-red, as if they had replaced the streetlights with globes of fear. In a haze that was both adrenaline-filled and remote, he surveyed the surrounding traffic while Mendel whimpered. Then he looked up. Something not human landed on the bridge. *Two* things shaped like writhing, tentacled slugs. He had to be losing his mind. Mendel howled.

He knew, as if the thought had been placed into his mind from an outside source, that he would remember none of this. No one who saw it would ever remember. No pictures would survive. Their film would be blank or full of innocuous scenes. Their minds would be in the same condition. But this was real. More real than anything he had ever encountered. How could he, the master of memory chemistry, not find a way to remember it? A smug consciousness emanated assurance that he would only remember what they wanted him to. He made a quick notation in his scheduler.

The next morning he couldn't have known that they had been right since he hadn't remembered it at all, although all of the neighbourhood dogs had all been howling that morning. But there was a new notation in his scheduler: *Wlk dg 7 p.m. Leif Pk 1 wk.* Walk the dog at seven p.m. in Leif Ericson Park for one week. For the life of him, he couldn't remember why he had written that. Was he supposed to meet someone there?

~~~

It was an academic atmosphere that tolerated the idiosyncrasies of all manner of geniuses, including biologists who refused to hurt animals in experiments. Not even the rats Dr Horatio had started with had been harmed.

Right now his research subjects were dogs, animals that had been rescued from a local shelter. They would not be injured by his procedures, and the dogs would all get good homes after they had given some value to science.

For now, the canines were just sharing each other's memories of a maze and some simple commands. One dog would learn the maze or command, and then his memory would be biochemically copied and added to the mind of another canine. The tests showed that his techniques were beginning to work very well indeed.

Horace peered two floors down through the blinds again and sighed. He could *not* understand why the animal rights protesters, who were finally going home for the weekend, had been outside of *his* clinic all this past week. His lab animals were all better off for having 'assisted' him. They received the best medical care and were spayed or neutered. They got lots of love when they were here and went on to carefully monitored adoptions. All of his dogs were fine. Except for the one at home. And that worried him.

Mendeleev was a shadow of his former, boisterous self. And so Dr Horatio Wright's scheduler now had an appointment for Mendel at the veterinarian's office. After work, Friday night, tonight. Directly after his scheduled walk in Leif Ericson Park.

~~~

The ringing of the telephone and the distant howling of neighbourhood dogs shook Horace out of a deep sleep the next morning. It was the veterinarian's office. He hadn't kept his appointment last night. Was something wrong? He sleepily apologized and promised to reschedule.

Groggy, he sat up and swung his feet to the floor, assailed then by a particularly severe wave of self-recrimination. How could he have neglected Mendel so? And what had he done last night that had been so important that he had forgotten to see the vet? The *quality* of his inability to remember frankly scared him. All he seemed to remember was some kind of vague pleasantness.

He was distracted by Mendel crying in his sleep. Something had been terrifying his poor dog all week, but this sound was soul-rending. He knelt down and shook the dog awake, then recoiled at the horror that was reflected in his best friend's eyes. He would give anything, *anything* to know what was bothering his dog so much. He hugged and petted Mendel for a moment and the animal stopped shaking.

Then he stopped stock-still as it hit him.

He could find out, or at least try to, with the set-up in his lab.

It would not be unusual for him to work on a Saturday, although the lab technicians would not be in, except for feedings and cage cleaning. So much the better. For what he was going to do was probably dangerous, and maybe just a little crazy. Instead of trying to transfer memory patterns biochemically between dogs he would attempt it between a dog and a human.

Who knew? Maybe Mendel would help him remember where he'd been last night. When he checked his appointment book to see if he was free to go to the lab today, he had another shock. He felt his heart pound and his face go white. There was just one entry, and he did not remember making it. It simply read, *Ask Mendel.*

"Mendeleev, umm, would you like to go for a ride?"

A tail thumped twice.

~~~

The security guard was used to Dr Horatio Wright bringing in stray dogs for his work on Saturday, which was his occasional 'star search' day at the animal shelter. Wally had never seen the Doc, as he called him, bring in Mendel, so for the guard, Mendeleev was just another mutt for the lab. The guard's shrug seemed to say, *Wet paw prints are the janitor's problem, not mine.*

A cacophony of happy barking greeted Horace's arrival. He put Mendel in a kennel run with a particularly friendly but strange-looking rescue dog they'd named Wilma. An Irish Setter/Shih Tzu mix, from the look of her, *And how had that ever happened?* he wondered. Mendel and she became immediate and enthusiastic friends. Horace left them to romp back and forth while he set up his apparatus.

When he adjusted the blinds to let in more light, he noticed a lone animal rights activist standing dejectedly outside in the persistent rain. Horace thought, *Why do this alone? I might need an assistant.* He lifted the security phone.

"Wally, could you escort that young protester inside for a tour of the lab? What? Oh, then lock up before you bring him up. What? Yes, I'll take full responsibility for him. But don't leave him alone with me unless I say you can. Thanks, Wally."

He went to the window and watched the umbrella-toting guard carry out his instructions. The young man's defiant pose gave way to wary surprise. The kid hesitated, seemed to ask Wally a couple of questions, shook his head, but then looked up. Horace smiled and waved down from the second story. The protester, rain streaming down his face, suddenly shrugged and then followed Wally inside.

What was it Isaac Asimov had said? Something like, "It's better to turn your enemy into a friend than to get rid of him." It was time to see if old Isaac was right.

A few minutes later Wally showed up with his charge: a soaked-to-the-skin, slim young man, perhaps in his late teens, who left a puddle wherever he stood. No doubt he was dressed all in black in an attempt at being dramatic, but in his present state it made him look somewhat like a soggy scarecrow, right down to his straw-coloured hair. His protest sign had, mercifully, been checked at the door.

Horace extended his hand. "Hello. I am Dr Horatio Wright. And you are?"

"Why'd you ask me up here?"

He lowered the proffered hand. "So you can see what it is we actually do here."

The young man glowered and swept his arm in an angry gesture that encompassed the whole lab. "I know what you do here. Hurtin' animals. Usin' them for experiments. They told me everything."

46

"Really? Who are *they*? And how do they know what we do here?" Horace kept his tone patient, reasonable. The young man remained silent and angry, looking at the cages as if for evidence to prove his point. Wally looked on impassively, leaning against the lab door.

Horace sighed. "Look, I'll make a deal with you, um . . . what did you say your name was?"

The angry eyes looked down. Silence. Wally-the-guard tapped his foot and cleared his throat.

"Jason."

"Okay, Jason. Here's the deal. I hope you know I took a big risk inviting you up here. I'm going to show you exactly what we do. And I want you to watch—"

"No way!"

"—and tell me if there's any way I can make my animals happier or more comfortable. And you can tell me all of the things you wanted to say while you were stuck out there in the rain. Otherwise, you go back outside right now. Deal?"

He was met with stunned silence. Then the young man found his voice. "You . . . do anything that might hurt an animal, and . . . I might try to make you stop."

Horatio nodded. "Sounds good to me." Then he extended his hand to the young man, again.

Belligerence melted into wary disbelief. "You're kidding, right?"

"Nope."

Jason looked hard at him for a moment. Then he extended a damp hand. "Okay, then. You got yourself a deal." They shook hands, eye-to-eye, solemnly. Horace kept his thoughts to himself.

Okay, Isaac. Wish me luck.

~~~

Horace's lab assistant called in sick. So he had Jason fill in, getting him to help with cage cleaning, feeding, and generally making a fuss over the dogs. All of which was under the watchful eye of Wally, until Horace was comfortable with the situation and the guard, with a doubtful backward glance, left to make his required rounds.

Slowly the former protester seemed to realise that this lab was *not* the house of horrors that he'd been expecting. In fact, he was shocked to realize that he was in the presence of a fellow animal lover. Patiently, Horace explained how he rescued the animals from the local shelter and took them to the vet, made sure they had all their shots and were spayed or neutered. But when he started to explain his experiments, Jason was wary and unimpressed.

"You've got no right doing that!" Jason said.

"But it does not really hurt them and could eventually help you to learn just by getting an injection. Less school, more results." Horace assured him. "And it could actually help us to communicate with other species, to understand how other species on this planet communicate with each other, how they think and feel. Don't you see?"

"I thought you said you would never do anything to these dogs you wouldn't do to yourself." Jason backed up a step, wary again.

"That is exactly right." Horace smiled.

"But you want to put a needle in their brains?"

"Yes. And today I am going to 'put a needle' into *my* brain, for one of them." He patted Mendel's cage.

Silence.

"You're pullin' my leg, right?"

"No, Jason. I'm quite serious. My best friend Mendel over here – he indicated which dog with a wave of his hand – has been having nightmares, and I want to know why. I'm going to try to transfer the memory of what is disturbing him to myself, to help him. Would you help me do that?"

The Adam's apple of Jason's neck bobbed up and down nervously. "Only if . . ."

"Only if what, Jason?"

". . . only if you do the same thing to me, too."

"No way, that's too risky. I am risking my job here but I work here. You're just a visitor. I will not risk you in any way." He pulled on his chin, hesitating. A decision was made. This fellow would do. "You can really help, though. I need someone other than myself to monitor this experiment, to do the notes and take observations." Horace gave him a steely look. "Are you up to that?"

Perhaps this was the first time that this young man had felt a part of something where he had the full confidence of an adult. "I think so. It's just a shot, kinda, and it's to try to help a dog, right? Maybe even help a lot of animals? Help stupid morons understand that animals have feelings, too? Make them understand that they got rights, just like people?"

Horace nodded. "We both want to help the dog, and other animals. We can try. If this works it ought to make people stand up and listen to what you have to say, yes. Yes, I certainly hope so, Jason.

"Here is what you'll need to do . . ."

If the experiment acted like the previous canine-to-canine transfers, they would not see results for 12 to 24 hours. The effect would then peak in three to five days. But of course, that was canine-to-canine. There was really no precedent for what Horace was about to attempt.

~~~

Five days later, they had their preliminary findings. The first definite result was that Dr Wright became quite certain of Mendel's favourite flavour of dog food. Horace hated liver, but now had warm memories of how good it tasted; in fact, he craved liver for the rest of the week. Then the reasons for Mendel's fears started to emerge, along with remembered scents and feelings foreign to human experience. The reason for Mendeleev's nightmares became more and more clear.

Slowly there had grown in Horace's awareness memories of a strong sense of menace. The cause if this menace was simply too incredible to believe.

Then some of his colleagues in mental health sciences mentioned to him over lunch that they had a recent run of hallucinating human patients reporting the same things he had gathered from Mendel. These patients all had an imbalance in their brain chemistry. They showed trace amounts of an altered human neurotransmitter that had an uncanny resemblance to the canine neurotransmitter that he had discovered and had the honour of naming: plethoronin. This was the common denominator, he decided, for plethoronin was normally only found in canine brains. He started himself on a light dose of it and found his senses subtly altered.

When the dogs started howling again that night, he had to resist the urge to join in. As the dogs sensed it, he also knew it for a certainty. *They* were coming. People must be warned.

~~~

"All right, so it looks like your fur ball is upset 'cause something bad, real bad, is about to go down," Jason nodded as he fingered a can of soda in the lab's break room. "Down by the bridge, near as you can tell." Jason pointed at Dr Wright's notes. "What it sounds like is —wow, this is weird — some sort of stuff that doesn't even belong on this Earth, or in this dimension? Anyhow you said it really felt like these things that are coming are dangerous. And all of this is because dogs can kind of see stuff we can't see?" It was a tolerable précis of his findings.

"Well put, Jason. But try explaining that at a scientific conference." Horace sighed. He scratched Mendel behind the ears as they sat alone at a table next to a humming kitchenette refrigerator. "That sixth sense some dogs seem to have about the paranormal does seem to be biochemical. And we have ample corroboration that this is not only Mendel's memory. Another three people with a plethoronin-like neurotransmitter were admitted to the hospital's psychology ward today, with what their doctors are calling 'that mass delusion.' The same scenario Mendel showed me. Too much of a coincidence." He glanced down at a discarded newspaper without really reading it. "Jason, *they* are planning something soon. Yet what can we possibly do about it? It's hopeless."

Jason grinned and reached down to pat Mendel. "You're still thinking like humans are all we've got on this planet. I dunno that *we* have to do much. Why don't we let Mendel and his buddies take care of things for us?" He jerked his thumb toward the dogs back in the lab. "This is their world, too." He leaned closer and lowered his voice.

"Just between you and me, my friends are planning a little jailbreak at the Bay Street dog pound tomorrow . . . but that probably wouldn't be enough. Hey!" he suddenly pointed at the paper. "Look at this, will ya?"

Horace read the article. It was a piece about *Dogs Walk Against Arthritis*, also scheduled for tomorrow. The annual summer charity event was to start in Ocean Park, and head toward the Verrazano-Narrows Bridge. Over one thousand dogs (and their owners) were expected to attend. He experienced a jolt of hope. "Jason. Do you think it's too late for Mendel and me to enter this? If I could just find a way to dose their owners with plethoronin . . ."

Jason was thoughtful. "Wait. I have an idea . . ."

~~~

Saturday was a scorcher, just like the weatherman had predicted. The hard part had been getting the canine neurotransmitter-laced bottles donated to *Dogs Walk Against Arthritis*, but he'd done that through a third party. Squinting into the sunset he could see that the water was nearly gone.

And as the last ray of light slid behind Staten Island, every dog at the event simultaneously pricked up its ears, and sat. Then the ear-splitting canine howling spread. Most of the dogs' owners stood there with wide eyes, suddenly sweating despite the cooling ocean breezes. Their dogs stood almost as one, straining at their leashes and looking back, growling and begging to be released. To run. To protect. To stand in the way of danger. To kill, if necessary. Horace held his breath.

It was obvious which owners had drunk the neurotransmitter-laced water. These people felt the threat too, somehow in synch with their dogs even as Horace was with his snarling Mendel. Whatever the menace was, the humans knew as surely as their dogs that it was *real*.

All cars on the busy bridge stopped, and the drivers that Horace could see all had blank unseeing expressions. A collective gasp ran through the tense crowd. They looked at an eerie, otherworldly light start at the lower level of the Verrazano, right by the toll booths. It outlined a widening rift in the night that was darker than the choppy Hudson. A sense of déjà vu permeated Dr Horatio Wright's brain as he finally *remembered* feeling this before. *Things* lumbered out of this rift – huge, menacing nightmares of slime and teeth that crushed cars as they flung them and their drivers out of their way.

With grim determination most of the dog owners followed his lead, unclipped their leashes, hugged their dogs but then urged them on.

People screamed. Street lights went out. Those trying to call 911 got an earful of static, then silence. The only other sounds were the crackling of hell-light around a gash in the universe, and Earth's growling defenders racing between the cars, to war.

Strange light shone on an arrow of baying, snarling dogs closing in, selflessly racing to meet the threat. More dogs, probably the escapees from the Bay Street pound, joined them from the other side of the bridge. There was a distant, inhuman scream as pit bulls, Dobermans, German Shepherds, Akitas and all manner of mixed-breeds set upon nightmares, fangs bared.

A few of the tentacled brutes started to fall under the wall of canine defenders.

The monsters seemed not to expect resistance and started to pull back. With alien bodies littering the bridge and over a thousand witnesses, their stealth was exposed; their attack defeated.

But Mendel came back and nosed Horace's hand. And suddenly, Horace had questions. He was filled with a courage that he did not understand. Horace, walking alone toward the bridge, stopped and faced one of the alien beings with Mendel at his side, growling low in the throat.

A voice twisted strangely in his head, like cold-speaking fog. *"You're aware. How? And we had no idea you had such fierce guardians, immune to our influence, and able to communicate with you. Our scouts told us that your dimension would be almost defenceless."*

Horace tried to answer in kind, *Well, not defenceless, obviously. You picked the wrong world.*

A pause. *"What do you call these defenders of your world?"*

We call them 'dogs' – or 'man's best friend'. Mendel bared his teeth and growled deeper in his throat.

The monster rolled the word around in its mind in a distaste Horace could feel it like a rope of thorns. *"Dogs,"* it spat. *"They know no fear. You share your world with these beings?"*

They are friends and partners in all regions of our world, yes. Horace felt his mind being probed by a slime of thought, which withdrew as if stung.

"I see that you speak the truth. We go. We shall not return. All that we request is that you call off these 'dogs'."

The retreat was not entirely civilized. When the creatures tried to pull their dead and wounded back with them, a few victorious, snarling dogs still stood sentry over the bodies.

~~~

No dog went through the rift – instead they backed away – but they growled and snarled at the retreating things until the rift glowed brighter and suddenly snapped shut. Like a pack of wolves, the dogs on the bridge circled and growled, then broke up and most of them started looking for their owners. Shouts of "Good dog!", "Good boy!" and "Good girl!" rang out as faithful companions limped or strutted back to their people.

Street lights flickered back on. Sirens wailed in the distance. Drivers awoke from their trances, confused and horrified. And the canine-linked humans on the ground started to cheer, as they ran toward the bridge, to check on their friends, their defenders, their fellow travellers on this Earth. Their dogs.

~~~

A month later, Dr Horatio Wright was walking Mendel in Leif Ericson Park after lunch. He was quietly satisfied with the news he had received that morning: Jason had been accepted into the school's veterinary medicine program thanks to his glowing letter of recommendation. It would be rewarding, Horace thought, to train a protégé.

As always, it was a toss-up deciding who was walking whom. Mendel pulled him hard, this time toward a bunch of skateboarders hanging out near a row of vendors selling brightly coloured kites rippling against a sapphire sky. A couple of the skaters backed up at Mendel's huge size, but mostly they were curious.

"Hey. Nice dog. Does he bite?"

Dr Horatio Wright pulled back, hard. "Sit, Mendel. Sit!" *Thud.* "They don't come any friendlier." Mendel sat panting with his tongue hanging out and blissfully had his ears scratched by his third group of strangers of the afternoon.

And all was right in their world.

WENDY S. DELMATER lives and breathes short fiction, both at *Abyss & Apex* magazine, the Hugo-nominated semiprozine she's run for over a decade, and on her hard drive. Somehow her stories occasionally break free and can be found in print.

The Stupefying Snailman, Gastropod of Justice versus The Disease that Steals the Soul

Ira Nayman

"Do you have any last words before I finally, finally, finally blast you into your constituent atoms?" The Cerulean Snort snorted.[1]

"You'll never get away with this, Cobalt Crustacean!" Snailman shouted defiance.

"It's, uhh, Snort, actually," the villain snorted. "The Cerulean Snort." It had long been a sore spot with The Cerulean Snort that all of the really good shades of blue had already been taken by other supervillains, heroes or one really popular restaurant chain[2].

"Close enough, Snert!"

"It's – oh, never mind."

DEAR LISA,

WE GET THROUGH IT AS BEST WE CAN. THERE'S ALWAYS LIGHT – DO YOUR BEST TO LOOK FOR IT.

Love

---

[1] How did our heroes get into their current scrape? You will know if you have read *The Stupefying Snailman, Gastropod of Justice* issue 637, "Don't Go In There, Snailman! It's a Trap!" On the other hand, you won't know if this is the first issue of the comic book you have ever bought; in that case, you really should find a copy of the previous issue before you go any further or none of what is about to happen will make the least bit of sense to you.

[2] As astute readers, or their grandparents, will remember from *The Stupefying Snailman, Gastropod of Justice* issue 13, "For What Is In a Name?"

The confrontation took place in one of the many large, abandoned warehouses that dotted CityTown; the warehouses made convenient hideouts for the city's supervillains during periodic outbreaks of their supervillainy. This one happened to be in Little Constantinople, a mythical area of CityTown where people were a little confused about their national heritage. The warehouse was three storeys of crumbling faith in economic progress and peeling paint, with a ring of windows just below the roof. On those occasions when light flashed from the windows accompanied by poorly muffled screams, citizens of Little Constantinople would shake their heads sadly and think, *Another superhero/supervillain confrontation? Ah, well, the superhero always wins, so he certainly doesn't need my help!* Then, they would put their hands over the ears of the young child who always seemed to be walking with them and hurry on to their destination on the other side of the neighbourhood.

In the middle of this vast, now temporarily unabandoned warehouse, The Stupefying Snailman, Gastropod of Justice, was strapped down in a large chair that looked like a metal Barcalounger. The chair was tilted at a forty-five-degree angle – the angle of utmost evil – the better to meet the tip of a huge laser-like device that was pointed directly at his face. Snailman's pink and grey tights were torn; confined as he was, his jet black cape was even more useless than it usually proved to be. His watery blue eyes darted this way and that, like the restless ocean in any shipwreck story.

In front of him, on a raised platform, The Cerulean Snort emoted triumphant. "I hope you appreciate that the seat on which you are currently immobilized has a back with a hole I can open to accommodate your shell," he snorted.

"Very thoughtful of you, fiend!" Snailman snappily replied.

"I try."

The Cerulean Snort wore his usual orange and black leotard (proving once again that supervillains who are colour-blind should not design their own costumes). The platform held the usual vast bank of impressive-looking control panels (although his threat usually came down to pushing a single large button or flipping an isolated switch somewhere in the middle). Off to one side, just outside the field of vision of Snailman's strapped-down head, Big Mac, the flatbed truck that was his transportation and friend, was held in a massive stasis field.

The weapon that was pointed between Snailman's eyes had been called The Atomic Vaporizer by The Cerulean Snort, and, since it was his device, nobody felt the need to argue with the appellation. In normal hands, a vaporizer is merely a method of enhancing the liquid content of the air in a room to help somebody deal with breathing problems. In the hands of a madman, a vaporizer is a machine of terror and destruction. The Atomic Vaporizer was lit up brighter than a Christmas tree in a burning fireworks factory in the middle of the afternoon.

The Cerulean Snort chuckled snortingly. Or, snorted chucklingly. He could be inscrutable that way. "How long I have dreamed of getting you this close to destruction! I thought for sure I had you that time in the abandoned warehouse on Leacock and Richler!"[3]

"What?" Snailman scoffed. "You mean, the time you dumped me in a vat of rabid guppies?[4] I didn't even break a sweat!"

"N . . . no. You're thinking of the confrontation we had at the abandoned warehouse on Doctorow and Sawyer."

"I think you're the one who is confused, here, Snort. That's the place you used your Dimensional Doorway™ to grab creatures from other dimensions to fight me in an Arena of Unpleasant Consequences!"[5]

---

[3] That confrontation occurred in *The Stupefying Snailman, Gastropod of Justice* issue 316, "Do I Look Funny to You? Do I Amuse You?"

[4] See *The Stupefying Snailman, Gastropod of Justice* issue 234, "A Fish Tale Even Herman Melville Wouldn't Tell" for all the finny details.

[5] Snailman might not recall these events quite as they happened, but you will if you read *The Stupefying Snailman, Gastropod of Justice* issue 376, "Of Squiggles and Squoggles and Things That Jump At You From the Right!"

The Cerulean Snort hesitated, confused. "I . . . don't own a Dimensional Doorway™. It seems like a neat idea, but it's just not mine."

"Snailman!" Big Mac shouted. "You're thinking of your seventh encounter with Mysterion, The Question Mark!"

"Thanks, Percy, but I think I know my own canon!"

While The Cerulean Snort was trying to come up with an original canon/cannon pun, Big Mac said, "Actually, it's Lashonda."

"Lashonda? Who is that?"

"Don't you remember, Snailman? Percy died when The Master Bildungsromaner caused a volcano to appear in the middle of CityTown! He heroically saved a pod of orphans who were visiting blind puppies at an animal shelter!"[6]

"Well, no – I mean, but, there's only ever been one Big Mac . . ."

"Actually, I'm the third. The first had a drug problem – he died in a bar fight!"[7]

"Who . . . who are you again?"

"Lashonda Shaniqua," Big Mac told him. "The plucky young dark-skinned girl from the ghetto whose soul was sucked out of her body by one of the seven Reality Rhinestones wielded by the demon Kal-Ip-Erse and placed in a flatbed truck?[8] Ever since, we've been looking for my body so that my spirit could be reunited with it – remember?"

"I – why do you sound like Percy?"

"Uhh, well, anybody speaking out of the speakers of a flatbed truck would probably have a tinny, metallic sounding voice!"

---

[6] As grief-stricken fans will remember from *The Stupefying Snailman, Gastropod of Justice* issue 600, "This Issue, a Hero . . . Sandwich Dies!" And what a tasty issue it was, too!

[7] *The Stupefying Snailman, Gastropod of Justice* issue 369, "Trouble Comes To Town, Has a Couple of Drinks, Spray Paints Something Nasty on City Hall and Passes Out in the Back of Yutz' Deli." What can I tell you? It was the eighties . . .

[8] This was part of an epic six issue story arc that was collected in the graphic novel called *The Dark Snail Returns*. The introduction of Lashonda Shaniqua was part of an effort to bring more racial and ethnic diversity to the characters in *The Stupefying Snailman, Gastropod of Justice*. Readers were divided on how successful making a flatbed truck a "black" character was at furthering the cause of diversity in comics . . .

There was a brief silence, into which The Cerulean Snort snorted: "Finished?" When there came no response, he continued: "Good. Now, where was I? Brought you to consciousness? Yes. Explained the workings of The Atomic Vaporizer in enough detail to give you some idea of how to thwart it? Check. Making final death threats. Right. Okay, then. Do you have any last words before I . . ." The Cerulean Snort trailed off. Snortingly. "No, I'm sorry, I can't do this," he waved a hand at Snailman. Then, he pressed a button on the control panel (other than the central, deadly one, I mean) and the light show slowly shut down.

"Wait, what—" Snailman was confused.

"What evildoing are you planning now?" Big Mac shouted for him.

"I'm letting you go."

The restraints that held Snailman to The Atomic Vaporizer slid open. "It's a trap!" Big Mac shouted. "Don't fall for it, Snailman!"

"Oh, I suppose I should let you go, too," The Cerulean Snort snorted. He pressed another button, this one on the far side of the control panel.

"Why are you doing this?" Big Mac shouted.

"Oh, please, lower your voice," The Cerulean Snort snorted. "The acoustics in this abandoned warehouse allow me to hear you perfectly well. Especially now that the machines are shutting down."

"Why are you doing this?" Big Mac politely asked.

"Look at him!" The Cerulean Snort snorted, waving a hand in Snailman's direction. The Gastropod of Justice was fingering the straps of The Atomic Vaporizer with wonder, as if he had never seen an evil villain's death machine before in his life. "He's obviously not at the top of his game. I could just kill you both, but what would be the fun in that? No, I think I'm going to go after the Fast Food League of America – a villain can always count on the Taco Belle to put up a good fight!"

"We should arrest your sorry patoot!" Big Mac grimly stated.

"Oh, don't be tiresome," The Cerulean Snort snorted. "Hello! Yoo hoo! Mister Stupefying!"

Snailman turned to face The Cerulean Snort. "I'm sorry. Are you talking to me?"

"Do you remember how to evoke your time dilation powers?"

Snailman looked surprised. "I have time dilation powers?"

The Cerulean Snort turned back towards Big Mac and snorted, "I have to pee. When I get back, you two better be out of my conveniently placed warehouse!"

As The Cerulean Snort made his way through a curtain behind the platform, Big Mac felt the stasis field holding him . . . her . . . it? Herit? Yes, he felt the force field – oh, wait . . . she . . . it? Sheit? Okay, I'm going to go with sheit, but let's not think too much about the word's potential other meanings – sheit felt the force field holding herit in place fade away. Sheit immediately drove to Snailman's side. He was standing over the chair in which he had recently been held captive.

"Will you look at that?" Snailman marvelled.

As the sound of liquid hitting porcelain tinkled in the background, Big Mac let down the panel at the back of herits (no point in going through all that again – you had to know where this would be heading) bed. "Quick!" Big Mac ordered. "Climb aboard so that we can get you home!"

Snailman slowly slithered onto the panel, leaving his patented Snailman slime on the floor of the warehouse. Big Mac started raising it just as the tinkling ended. But then the tinkling started again and the truck sighed in relief. "Strap yourself in!" sheit advised.

As Snailman strapped himself in, he looked at the belts embedded in the floor of the truck and wondered, "Heeeey, when did you get these, Mac?"[9] Sheit, hearing a flushing sound, didn't have time to respond. Big Mac smashed through one of the warehouse doors and made herits way into the night.

"What's all the noise?" The Cerulean Snort snorted as he emerged from behind the curtain. When he saw the damage to the door, he snorted to himself, "I would have opened that if you had just asked me . . ."

~~~

"I think you should see a doctor," Big Mac advised.

---

[9] Of course, anybody who has read *The Stupefying Snailman, Gastropod of Justice* issue 612, "Snail Overboooooooaaaaaaard!" already knows the answer to that question.

"Pfeh!" Snailman scoffed. "I don't have time to see a doctor. The Cerulean Snort is threatening CityTown, and I have to find out where he's based before any more innocents suffer!"

"See, this is what I'm talking about."

"What are you talking about?"

"We just fought The Cerulean Snort!"

"Oh, well, we're here, so it must have gone well. Is he in jail, or—"

Big Mac regretted not having arms sheit could throw up in exasperation. "He let us go out of pity!"

"Oh, please! How many times have I kicked his wrongly coloured costumed ass? Why would he pity me?"

"That's what I want you to go to the doctor to find out!"

Big Mac had taken Snailman to the Snail Shellter, his crime-fighting headquarters built in the soft loam underneath Wesleydale Manor, alter-ego billionaire playboy Ryan Dervish's mansion. The room was a football field wide and a baseball infield high. There was a desk girded with a battalion of computer screens and keyboards, a supercomputer towering nearby. There was a workbench next to that and various mechanical devices scattered around the space. There were also objects that people who were fortunate enough to have been allowed into the Snail Shellter – only 4,337 as of the most recent issue – presumed to be artefacts of Snailman's adventures, but they weren't actually canon: one issue, they just appeared in the Snail Shellter. Some stayed, some didn't. There was a three-storey-tall Canadian nickel (the one in Sudbury was counterfeit; *The largest slug in the world*, Snailman always thought with a chuckle). There was the three-foot-tall green alien finger in a jar (at least, everybody always assumed that it was a finger . . .). Hanging on one wall was a framed deck of cards with superheroes on the back that supervillains used to keep track of whom they had conquered (Snailman was insulted that he was only the three of diamonds, but at least he wasn't the deuce – that dubious distinction fell on Tautology Man). Then, there were the objects that were harder to identify . . .

When he first started using the underground lair, the floor was covered with snails. Snailman didn't mind the crunching sounds every time anybody walked in the room, but the accumulation of snail guts made parts of the floor quite slippery. This had unfortunate effects. The first time he blindfolded the first love of his life (in superhero guise, at any rate), Lainey Lippowitz, and brought her to the Snail Shellter, she slipped and hit her head on a bronze butterfly. "Oy, if I get a concussion out of this, I'm suing, Mister Snailman, sir!" she threatened. "You just see if I don't!"[10]

Dervish loved her all the more for it. Still, in order to avoid a lawsuit, he lined the edge of the floor of the Snail Shellter with low-level air vibrators that didn't affect people but kept his crustacean cousins climbing the walls.

Snailman sat at his desk. On three of his computer screens, newsfeeds and data streamed incomprehensibly. On the fourth screen, an episode of *Family Guy* streamed incomprehensibly. Big Mac was in the bay built especially for herit, getting checked over by automated systems. "Are you feeling well-oiled this afternoon, Master Mac?" the bay asked in a comforting voice, the voice of an American actor doing a British accent. Fortunately, neither Snailman nor Big Mac had ever spoken to somebody with a real British accent so they couldn't challenge the voice's authenticity.

"Yes," Big Mac replied. "But, I wish you'd call me Lashonda, Jeevis."[11]

"I shall endeavour to keep that in mind, Master Mac," Jeevis deferentially responded. "In the meantime, I couldn't help but notice a gash in your passenger-side door. Shall I just fix that up for you?"

While Big Mac suffered the indignity of nanobots filling the scrape in herits chassis, Snailman discovered an object in his hand. It was round, with a flat bit at the bottom. It was orange. *Ah*, Snailman thought, *this must have something to do with what happened this afternoon. I'll just* . . . He searched his desk, but couldn't find what he was looking for.

---

[10] The scene was a bit of comic relief in the otherwise bleak *The Stupefying Snailman, Gastropod of Justice* issue 215, "Enter Spandex Man!"

[11] Fans who gave up on *The Stupefying Snailman, Gastropod of Justice* 15 issues ago will not be aware that Jeevis was the name given to the AI that ran the Dervish household and the Snail Shellter after Thursday Past, the AI that previously ran the Dervish household and the Snail Shelter, heroically gave its . . . well, not life, obviously, but existence in the battle against Stegasaurus Man. Thanks for giving us another chance!

"Where is my Mauritz confabulator?" Snailman turned to the vehicle bay and asked accusingly. The Mauritz confabulator was a device Ryan Dervish had the science division of Whirling Enterprises create; it revealed the past twenty-four hours of an object. Because the fatal flaw in his power was that he moved slowly, he often had to use the device to replay events to better understand what had happened.

"How should I know?" Big Mac answered shortly.

"You must have moved it somewhere."

"I didn't touch your Maury Povitchulator!"

"Mauritz confabulator! You had to move it because I wouldn't have!"

"Why would I move your whosy whatsis?"

"Mauritz confabulator! Maybe you picked it up while you were dusting and put it down in a different place!"

"Ryan! I'm a two-ton truck! Do I strike you as somebody who gives a shit about dust?"

"But—"

"Where did you last see the device?"

"I always keep it to the right of my keyboard," Dervish grumbled. He patted a point on the desk that was obviously empty.

"That's not what I asked you. Where do you remember seeing it last?"

"Don't mess with me, Mac!" Snailman shouted. "I been a superhero since you were just a gleam in an assembly worker's eye! If I had put the goddam Mauritz confabulator on the work bench next to the supercomputer, don't you think I would have remembered that I had put the goddam Mauritz confabulator on the work bench next to the – oh." Snailman looked over at the workbench next to the supercomputer and was embarrassed by what he found there.

"Yeah. Oh." Because sheit was communicating out of a terrible truck radio, sheit couldn't express a wide range of emotions, but sarcasm was universal. "I've got to go to work," sheit informed Snailman. In herits civilian identity, Big Mac hauled construction equipment for Sandoz and Son. "Remember: you've got the Alzheimer's Fundraiser this evening."

"Yes, I remember," Snailman said. After a couple of seconds, he sheepishly added: "Where is it again?"

Big Mac backfired – sheit's version of a sigh.

"You need to see a doctor, Ryan. I'm worried that our run-in with The Mnemonicist last month has affected your mind."

Snailman snorted. "The Mnemonicist hit *you* with his fancy-schmancy gun, not me."

"Yeah, but I'm a magical creation whose memory resides . . . well, we don't really know where, but certainly not in a human brain, so nothing The Mnemonicist could do would affect me. But, some of the ray may have bounced off me and affected you."

"I don't wanna talk about it," Snailman mumbled.

"Ryan, if—"

"I don't wanna talk about it!" Snailman roared.

"This is not over," Big Mac assured him, and slowly drove up the ramp that led to the holograph of a rabbit warren that masked the ground level entrance to the Snail Shellter.

"Yeah, yeah." Snailman waved a dismissive hand at Big Mac's rear fender.[12]

------

[12] This encounter with The Mnemonicist was shown in *The Stupefying Snailman, Gastropod of Justice* issue 634, "You Must Remember . . . You . . . Remember . . . This? That? The Other? Umm . . . Somebody Must Something, Something . . ." If you don't remember the issue, it may be because it was rumoured to have a misprint, and the entire million copy print run was bought by seven collectors trying to find any issue that may have contained it (if one did, he isn't saying). There may be a cache of copies buried somewhere in Alamogordo, New Mexico, but they are probably no longer readable. Why don't we let Snailman explain what hap – no, he said he didn't want to talk about it, didn't he? Umm, okay, I guess it's up to me to give you the broad outlines of what happened.

The Mnemonicist (civilian name: Mem Rory M. Plante) was born with the power to implant false memories into people's heads; he had created the Mnemosyne Pistol to focus the memories and direct them at his intended victims. The false memories weren't long, and most often had the quality of YouTube videos about beloved pets. This made them more confusing than anything, but the confusion didn't give The Mnemonicist time to do anything more evil than swipe candy from grocery store displays. Worse, because the memories that were implanted into his victims originally belonged to The Mnemonicist himself, they gave Snailman enough information to track the not especially super villain down. Plante was convicted of twelve counts of petty theft, fined $500 dollars and put on probation for six months. He decided he wasn't cut out for a life of crime and eventually opened a store exclusively selling computer storage.

Sixteen years later, wealthy CityTownians started taking money out of their bank accounts, but had no memory of doing so and no idea where the money went. Not having any leads, Snailman called upon Plante for some advice, since he was an expert on memory. The next thing he knew, Snailman was in an abandoned warehouse in what

"Shall I prepare your tuxedo for this evening's soiree, Mister Snailman, sir?" Jeevis asked.

"Yes, please," Snailman said.

"I should remind you, sir, that the benefit starts in three hours, seventeen minutes. If you want to be ready for it, you will have to leave the Snail Shellter no later than twenty-six minutes from now."

"Yeah. Thanks."

---

would prove to be the Inuit neighbourhood of CityTown. (As it happened, the area taken up by the warehouse was larger than the area of the neighbourhood around it; fortunately, this is not a story about urban zoning regulations, so we don't have to try to explain *that*.) Plante was wearing his Mnemonicist costume (black, with tiny pink brains forming an M on the chest), which was a bit snug in the waist, but otherwise fit him quite well after all that time.

Thinking he had all the time in the world, The Mnemonicist explained that he had reversed the polarity of the Mnemosyne Pistol (a trick he had learned watching reruns of an old science fiction television programme). It was still early days, of course, but he found that *removing* people's memories was a lot more effective than implanting false ones. You know, money accumulation-wise and stuff. What he hadn't realized was that Snailman had activated the Snail Signal the moment he had regained consciousness. It projected an image of a snail into the night sky, which would alert Big Mac to the fact that he was in trouble; the truck would then follow a homing device in his costume and rescue the Gastropod of Justice. In good time. Eventually. The Snail Signal appeared to assemble the image in the sky one photon at a time. Honestly, it made John Cage's song "AS SLOW AS POSSIBLE" SEEM RUSHED.

FORTUNATELY, JEEVIS HAD REDESIGNED THE SNAIL SIGNAL ACTIVATION DEVICE SO THAT IT AUTOMATICALLY WARNED BIG MAC ABOUT SNAILMAN'S DANGER. (THE COMPUTER NANNY RETAINED THE IMAGINE IN THE SKY AS A KIND OF PERFORMANCE ART.) THUS, The Mnemonicist got to the part of his story where he first became aware that he could fulfill his childhood dream of becoming a supervillain – and, wouldn't Miss Skurlingsohn, his grade three Philosophy of Evil teacher, be proud of him? – when Big Mac burst through the wall of the abandoned warehouse. Out of reflex, The Mnemonicist turned to fire at the truck that was barrelling towards him. The shot harmlessly bounced off the vehicle's front bumper (or, not so harmlessly, if you believe the theory that it bounced off Big Mac and hit Snailman instead). In any case, Mac sideswiped The Mnemonicist, knocking the gun out of his hand. As he put his wrists together in anticipation of being arrested, the supervillain philosophically remarked, "It was fun while it lasted . . ."

Snailman turned the object over in his hand, but his enthusiasm for subjecting it to the Mauritz confabulator had dissipated with his argument with Big Mac. He knew something was wrong, but he wasn't certain what it could be. With a sigh, he put the object down on the table and made his way to the snailevator that would take him up to the library in his mansion. The trip up the five floors took only three minutes, seventeen seconds. Unfortunately, getting to his bedroom suite, which was poorly placed at the opposite end of the mansion, took over an hour. Of course, that problem could be solved easily by building a second snailevator in his bedroom, but other things would intervene before he could think of doing it . . .

~~~

The grand ballroom of Wesleydale Manor was at least as big as the ballroom of the Overlook Hotel, but lacking the latter's buckets of blood and sense of impending doom; this tended to make it a somewhat more festive place.

Ryan Dervish stood suavely in the middle of the room, surveying the curdled cream of CityTown's high society. Dervish wore a tuxedo specially tailored to minimize the silhouette of the shell on his back. It wasn't that people weren't aware of it; enough images of him playing tennis at the country club or participating in a high-wire act in tights and a T-shirt at a Cirque de Oy Vey fundraiser for disfigured circus performers had appeared in the press that his shell was hard to avoid. He just didn't want to call attention to it; this night wasn't about him.

The current love of his life, Linda Limpopo, walked up to him and handed him a tall glass. "Your water and soda," she said, then sipped her rum and Coke Zero.

After the death of the first love of his life, Lainey Lippowitz,[13] Dervish hit the bottle pretty hard. When it refused to shatter, he decided to drink its contents, instead. Unfortunately, it was tequila, and the mandatory salt around the rim almost killed him. If it hadn't been for a chance meeting with a Polynesian liposuctionist who dreamed of a career as a political cartoonist for a major metropolitan newspaper, Dervish's career as a gastropod of justice might have been cut tragically short.

___

[13] As readers of *The Stupefying Snailman, Gastropod of Justice* issue 332, "Noooooooooooo!" will never be able to forget. Nor will we let them, as that issue is the most reprinted of

"Did you hear what the President had to say about drone strikes in Texas?" Limpopo, who wore a tastefully slinky black dress that accentuated her substantial curves, asked.

"I . . . I've been kind of busy," Dervish replied. "You know, organizing this and . . . doing other things."

Limpopo nodded her perfectly round head. She didn't bother telling him the cartoon idea she'd recently had because political humour is lost on people who aren't familiar with the underlying issue. The pair drank for a moment, then Limpopo said, "Ryan, sweetie, remember the time I thought you were Snailman!"

Dervish nearly jumped out of his shell.[14] "Whu . . . what made you think of that?" he replied with all the nonchalance of a puppy in front of a firing squad.

"Oh, honey, don't worry," Limpopo laid a reassuring hand – well, a hand that she had meant to be reassuring, in any case – gently on his chest. "I was convinced by the video of you shaking hands with Snailman, even if you seemed to have a slight blue tint around your body."

"Oh. Well. Ahh . . ."

"I will admit that I did think it odd that you and Snailman were the only two people with shells in all of CityTown. But, your explanation that there is a tribe of shelled people in Belgium was totally convincing, even if you always keep putting off taking me there to meet your people."

"Well. Ahh. Oh . . ."

"Anyway, when Robert Smiley, Jr. told *Entertainment Tonight* that he had met the two of you and that you were both very charming – even if Snailman is taller – what last shreds of doubt that remained were completely banished."[15]

---

all Snailman comics. Not that we have to – even people who have never read *The Stupefying Snailman* shudder when they hear the name Lainey Lippowitz, even if they don't know why.

[14] Can you blame him? See *The Stupefying Snailman, Gastropod of Justice* issue 607, "This Title Under Construction" for all the tension and well-intentioned, but emotionally devastating if revealed deceit!

[15] *ibid*, which, I am told, is Sanskrit for, "Look, I've already told you once!" Smiley Jr. owed Dervish a huge favour for ensuring he got the lead in *Snailman: The Movie*. Until

"Then, why did you bring it up!" Dervish politely shouted.

"Just making fundraising ball conversation," Limpopo winked and kissed him on the cheek.

Before Dervish could respond, Mayor Frod, a genial blob of a man, walked up to Dervish and asked, "Hey, Ryan, how's it hanging?"

"We haven't put any new paintings on the walls for several years, Guillaume."

Mayor Frod looked at Dervish like his head had sprung antennae, his skin had turned green and his mouth had proposed that they find someplace quiet for a little anal probing. The Mayor frequently thought in body-part metaphors, one of the earthy qualities that had endeared him so to voters. He decided that Dervish was just making a little joke (an easy decision to make considering the size of his donation to the Mayor's campaign) and burst out laughing.

"That's what I love about you," Mayor Frod roared, "your quick wit!" He made to slap Dervish on the back, then thought better of it: the last time he had done it, the Mayor had to wear a cast on his hand for three weeks.

"Ahh. Well. Oh . . ." Limpopo smiled indulgently.

Lowering his voice, Mayor Frod, who decided not to bother pointing out that his first name was actually Budgerigar, asked, "Ryan, have you given any more thought to my proposal?"

"Your proposal?" Dervish evenly responded.

"That's right. We spoke about it in my office last week."

"Ah, that proposal." Dervish closed his eyes and smiled indulgently as he desperately tried to remember being in His Honour's office the previous week. Eventually, he opened his eyes and responded with a broad smile, "I'm sorry, Gernsback, but what you proposed is complicated, with a lot of possible repercussions – I'll need more time to study it."

"Of course," Mayor Frod replied, his smile getting less beamy at every incorrect use of his name. "Still, the window of opportunity is closing – I'll need your response as quickly as you can give it. Say, three o'clock tomorrow morning?"

---

then, Smiley Jr. was merely an actor with a reputation for being able to portray great emotional range and depth.

"It's a pleasure doing business with you, Mister Mayor."

Not reassured, Mayor Frod replied, "And, you." Then, he added, "Oh, look. There's my . . . sister's chiropodist! I have to say hi . . ." and walked away.

"Do you have any idea what the Mayor was proposing?" Limpopo asked.

Dervish smiled but didn't respond.[16]

Many drinks, speeches and even bites of food later, Limpopo was lecturing Dervish on the timeless appeal of Walt Kelly's *Pogo* when a – what would the redheaded equivalent of 'blonde bombshell' be? Red . . . knock 'em dead head? Let's say she had hair the colour of blood and envy, and eyes the colour of lasers. The woman was big-bosomed but relatively normally proportioned for a superhero story. She had cheekbones so sharp that suitors had to take five minutes before kissing her to determine the angle of approach to her lips least likely to get them cut.

"Lainey?" Dervish asked in disbelief.

"Who you talking to, sweetie?" Limpopo asked.

"Can't you see her? She's standing right in front of us!"

"Who's the bimbo?" Lainey Lippowitz asked.

"Lana's not a bimbo!" Dervish retorted.

Limpopo's eyes narrowed. "Who's calling me a bimbo?"

Too late, Dervish realized that this was not a discussion he wanted any part of. "Oh, uhh, nobody, honey. I, uhh, must have had too many . . . water and sodas . . ."

Limpopo concentrated her gaze on the point in front of them that Dervish had indicated. Something seemed to slowly come into focus. "Wait, there *is* somebody! It's a woman. A woman who is big bosomed but relatively normally proportioned for a superhero story. Hair the colour of blood and envy and eyes the colour of lasers. Cheekbones so sharp that suitors had to take five minutes before kissing – oh, my god, it's Lainey Lippowitz!"

"Are you . . . dating this woman?" Lippowitz demanded. "You two-timing rat!"

---

[16] Don't look at me – I'm not getting between two of the most powerful people in CityTown!

"You . . . you're dead!" Dervish responded.

Lippowitz put her hands on her hips, a pose that heroes generally used to signal that they were ready to take on all comers, and that women used . . . to signal more or less the same attitude, actually. "You should know better! In a universe with superheroes, nobody ever dies forever! I can't believe you found somebody else without thinking through all of the consequences of your actions!"

"I know, right?" Limpopo jumped in before Dervish could defend himself. "You'd think that somebody who moves so slowly wouldn't be able to decide things so quickly!"

"It's been twelve years," Dervish weakly stated.

"I don't envy you," Lippowitz told Limpopo. "Ryan can be sweet, but he's high maintenance."

"Tell me about it!" Limpopo responded. "When I oil his shell—"

Lippowitz squealed. "Ewww! He gets you to do that, too?"

"It's unhealthy when it gets too greasy!" Dervish protested.

"I will give him this: there is one area where Ryan's . . . slowness is a plus," Lippowitz stated.

"Mmm. A big plus," Limpopo agreed.

"A big . . . slow . . . plus."

"Mmmmmmmmm . . ."

The women burst out laughing.

It was for situations just like this that Snailman had built The Fortress of Saltitude close to the South Pole, as far away from humanity as it was possible to get.[17] Unfortunately, at the ribbon cutting ceremony for its opening, he realized that salt was deadly to snails and he could never go in. Later, he heard that some other superhero had squatted on his architectural achievement. Good luck to him! With the polar ice caps melting because of global climate change, it was only a matter of time before it fell into the ocean!

". . . slathers on the body like it was cocoa butter and he had just come out of a frying pan!" Lippowitz was saying.

---

[17] See *The Stupefying Snailman, Gastropod of Justice* issue 184, "It's Not Easy Being Slimy."

"Have you ever been around him before he showered?" Limpopo was replying. "He smells like dreams of an ocean voyage in the middle of a raging storm!"

"You know, kid, you're all right!"

"You're not so bad yourse—"

With a loud *SKEREEEE SHOOOOP!* the ceiling of the ballroom was peeled away. A huge square head with strange appendages on either side looked in.

"Is this a private party," the head boomed, "or can anybody attend?"

"What are you doing here, hockey stick head?" Dervish, grateful for the distraction, challenged the huge figure.

"It's Gargantuas, actually," Gargantuas pouted. Boomingly. Then, his face brightened. "Alzheimer's research is a worthy cause. I returned to Earth as soon as I heard in case there was any way I could lend a hand."

"The last time anybody heard from you, you were trying to eat the solar system!" Limpopo pointed out.[18]

"What can I say," Gargantuas boomed, grinning. "My eyes were too big for my stomach!"

He assured everybody that the only things he was interested in devouring were the waitresses in butterfly costumes. Gargantuas immediately started chatting up a petite blonde trying to circulate with a tray of shrimp puffs.

Warily watching Gargantuas Dervish thought, *This is surreal! Goodness, but I haven't experienced anything like this since the sixties!*[19] *What could possibly happen next?*

"Next patient of the day. Come on everybody, shuffle in. You've all been on buses in this city – any hint of shyness should have been squeezed out of you on your first trip. Now, anybody want to tell me the latest about Mister . . . Derbish?"

"Doctor Kassa, isn't that billionaire industrialist playboy, Ryan Dervish?"

---

[18] As recounted in *Infinite Crossover Wars*, issue 12, "Then, What?"

[19] See, for example, *The Stupefying Snailman, Gastropod of Justice* issue 62, "The Rabbit, The Hole and The Following Down." But, that's just one example of many. Really. The whole psychedelic thing happened, like, practically every other issue! And, no, I don't think the fact that it was the 1960s is a sufficient excuse!

"Sorry – I skipped breakfast and am feeling a little peckish. Thank you for volunteering, Smithson."

"Actually, it's Johnson."

"If I was a cruise ship director, I'm sure I'd care. So, what can you tell me about Mister *Derbish*'s condition?"

"Right. Well, the patient is in the final stage of Alzheimer's Disease. He has lost the ability to use language, which means it is no longer possible for him to communicate with the world outside of his head. We have no idea what's going on in there, but considering how rapidly his ability to access recent memories deteriorated, it would seem to be a reasonable assumption that there isn't much."

"Okay. That's how we got here. So, now what?"

"Uhh, eventually his brain won't be able to control his autonomic nervous system, and his vital organs will start malfunctioning. At that point, if nobody has given a resuscitation order, he will . . . well, die."

"Let that be a lesson to all of you. No matter how billionaire industrialist playboyey you are, when your time is up, you time is up. Is there anything we can do for him?"

"The only—"

"Oh, let's not always see the same hands. Gudrun! You haven't said anything for the last couple of rounds – you must be bursting with the joy of knowledge!"

"What can we do for the patient?"

"Quit stalling by repeating the question back to me!"

"Well, nothing. Make him as pain-free and comfortable as possible and let the disease take its course."

"I knew you had it in you. Now, if there's nothing else—"

"Doctor Kassa?"

"Yeeeesss?"

"Does the flatbed truck that's been parked out front of the hospital have anything to do with the patient?"

"How would I know?"

"It started appearing on the street after he was admitted."

"What do I look like: a traffic cop? If it doesn't have anything to do with his medical condition, I could care less. And, yes, before any of you say another word, I know that the phrase is actually 'I couldn't care less'. I was being ironic!"

"What an amazing thing the human mind is . . ."

"Yeah. It's constantly finding new ways to mess up its owner. Let's get on to the next patient.

As the private room in the hospital emptied, the figure on the bed smiled benignly at nobody in particular.

IRA NAYMAN had a thriving career as a species of small marsupial that lives in Australia before he became a writer. Since those heady days of his youth, he has self-published six collections of Alternate Reality News Service articles (available at better Amazons near you . . . r computer) and had three Transdimensional Authority novels published by Elsewhen Press. *Les Pages aux Folles* (http://www.lespagesauxfolles.ca), Ira's website of political and social satire, recently celebrated its thirteenth anniversary of weekly updates. Yes, it's all very exciting, the life of an international high-stakes satirist, but if you see Ira get a far-away look in his eye, know that he's dreaming of those long ago days when he ate leaves and his only concern was how long he should scratch his butt . . . "The Stupefying Snailman, Gastropod of Justice versus The Disease That Steals the Soul" was written in memory of Ira's grandfather, Bill, who lost his battle with Alzheimer's.

Another Reboot
Russ Bickerstaff

Mike was trying to impress Rachel. This didn't bother Tim. What bothered him was the fact that Mike *was* impressing Rachel. Really, there's no reason why Mike should have been as effective as he was. All he was doing was inverting gravity. And not even all the way either. Just playing with it. Just tickling it. Just a little bit of weightlessness. Nothing more than that. It wasn't like he was doing anything big or epic. And under the circumstances, there were far more impressive things that could have been done.

Tim had played with friction. Then bounced around atoms. He had created small civilizations and watched them die out. He was very active. He *wasn't* trying to impress anyone. He felt as though by virtue of that he probably should. And if he was going to impress anyone, he should definitely probably be impressing Rachel. She was amazing. She was gorgeous. (He had always liked her.) She could appreciate the things he was doing the way no one else could. She'd always make a point of saying so in such a nice way before Steve found the switch. Mike and Rachel were floating around all weightless. They were giggling like it was something new. They were acting like they couldn't have done that before the switch. When Steve had found that switch it changed everything. He shared it with all of them. He was such a nice guy. It's a pity what happened to him. (Or at least what they thought happened to him.) He could not have known what happened when they flipped that switch. He knew it was going to start all over, but who knew what was going to happen *then?* The entire history of everything erased and reset. Completely rebooted. Steve said it was gonna happen. (He knew *that much.*) Steve said that there was a good chance that they would be gods. We restart everything and we're there. Just a half a dozen of us: Steve and a few of his friends.

If you're there when everything gets reset you're part of it all. If you're there closing the door on one reality and opening the door on the next there's a good chance you're all going to be gods. That's what Tim was in it for. But not in some weird power trip. Not in some sense of really actually wanting to impress people. He was in it for the sense of exploration. For the adventure. He was there to feel it start all over. (Okay, yes: and become a god. But not because of the power.) Tim wanted to become a god because it was something to do. Because it was something that would create a larger connection with everything. And everyone would understand.

There they were trying to start something over in a truly dramatic way. And there were Mike and Rachel lightly floating like they didn't understand the full significance of what was going on. Rachel should have. Tim *knew* Rachel had to understand the full significance of what was going on. Tim had always thought that she seemed very bright. That she seemed very smart. She seemed like exactly the type of person who would be attracted to somebody like him. That she was exactly the type of person to be attracted by somebody like Tim. That's what he wanted. Not that he wanted to actively pursue it. Just that he wanted her to realize that that's what she wanted.

He didn't want to force her to be impressed with him. He didn't want to will her affection into being. Of course, having thoughts like this while being a god might have caused that to happen. He was fully aware of his desires, but he wasn't going to act on them. He had certain impressions about him. He had a certain idea of who he was that he wanted to uphold. And he wasn't the type of guy to go in for cheap ways to impress a girl like her. Not that she would've fallen for that sort of thing. Or at least not that she would've fallen for that sort of thing by someone like him. Not that she would've been impressed by that sort of thing by someone like Tim.

Evidently she was impressed with that sort of behaviour and someone like Mike, though. It was strange how they all kept their bodies. In retrospect, it kind of made sense. You didn't step into godhood lightly. And it certainly you didn't step into godhood without wanting to maintain full control of your sense of self. And the easiest way to do that for most people is to simply hang onto their bodies. However, Mike was a mesomorphic guy who was six and a half feet tall and Tim was a scrawny guy with bad eyesight, unfortunate hair and bad posture that was something he inadvertently ended up holding onto into the next reality. Rachel was drop-dead gorgeous.

Rachel and Mike continued to float. And it's not like Tim wanted it to happen or anything. It's not like he specifically planned it. But it's not like he specifically planned it with Steve either. It just sort of happened. Two of them. One of him. Everything else that was the all of everything. As such a shock and a sudden splattering. The one of him. Everything else that was the all of everything. As such a shock and a sudden splattering. Great gobs of everything squished out in all directions as the fabric of every conceivable dimension and direction oozed into every other dimension and direction causing quantities and quantification to bleed into an amorphous liquid that rapidly evaporated into pure potentiality on the other side of everywhere.

There was utter silence. No giggling. There was only stillness at twilight. Tim tried to animate them again. They seemed limited. They seemed strange shadows of themselves. But then, they always did. They always seem like something less than people. So maybe there were no different. Maybe this happened before. Maybe he'd started it all over and got Steve to find the switch. Maybe it had happened countless times and he simply forgot.

Tim sat and watched the sunset. Or he sat and watched the sunrise. He sighed into the moment waiting for the switch to come, waiting for the switch to happen one more time. The gentle flipping. Everyone coming back again and then disappearing into some strange shadow of potentiality. He could feel it. Feel the potential of everything resting on the threshold of the now.

RUSS BICKERSTAFF is a professional theatre critic and aspiring author living in Milwaukee, Wisconsin, US, with his wife and two daughters. Last year, his short fiction appeared in over 30 different publications, including *Hypertext Magazine, Pulp Metal Magazine, Sein und Werden,* and *Beyond Imagination.* His Internarrational Where Port can be found at http://ru3935.wix.com/russ-bickerstaff

Pipes
Margaret Karmazin

"So, are you adjusting?" asked Simpson. "Saw you talking to that sexy little assistant manager in Zebang's. Got something going there?"

Lou blushed. Though his hair was dark, he was cursed with light, flushing skin. "I like her," he said.

"You know, I don't have anything to back up what I'm saying," said Simpson, "but I heard a rumour that she is undercover police."

"That can't be true," said Lou. "She seems just what she is."

Simpson snorted. "No one on Ganymede Station is exactly what they seem, my friend. In fact, this whole enterprise isn't what it seems."

"What do you mean?"

Simpson moved closer. "Why they built this space can in the first place — you don't know, do you?"

"Well, *tell* me," said Lou.

Simpson glanced around though there was no one tangled in the pipes but themselves. "The walls have ears . . ."

"What, they're bugged?"

"Probably not, but you never know. I'll bet you think they built this enterprise just out of humankind's sense of adventure." His long brown eyes danced with sardonic merriment.

~~~

Lou Slezak's Uncle Chaz had run a highly successful plumbing and heating business in Edison, NJ and after the ocean rose and flooded parts of the coast, he contentedly retired and moved to Colorado. He would not have believed, if he had lived long enough, that his nephew would carry on his legacy 390,400,000 miles from Earth. But that is what can happen when you have an astronaut for a cousin.

"Engineers designed the system, but we need plumbers to help keep it going on a regular basis. Very special ones, of course," said the cousin who had made four trips to Mars and back. He went on for some time describing the thrills of space travel.

Lou listened; he was good at listening, something his ex only now appreciated since she had remarried a pushy extrovert. "Are you kidding?" he said. "You think I'd shut down my lucrative business and comfortable life to go live in spartan hell on some space station?"

"You don't get it," said David. "This new station isn't going to be any spartan hell. They've been working on it, if you've been paying attention, for nine years and it's probably the highest achievement of humankind – far superior to those questionable attempts at a Martian colony. Take a virtual tour! You'll be amazed. Like a top of the line cruise ship, you'll see."

"It smacks of military," said Lou. "I've watched my brother's stint in that realm, all that bomb building and dismantling and how he has no personal life to speak of and no thanks."

"Military? Sure, there'd be some ranking on the station but believe me, it wouldn't be anything like what you're thinking. You'd have R and R, time for a personal life and no bombs!" David laughed.

"Meh," said Lou, about to wave his hand dismissively, but David stopped him. "How many times have I heard you say you're bored, even with commercial work, and wish something more interesting would come along? You've taken several classes in electronic plumbing, right? Haven't I heard you say that you wish you had a mission in life?"

"Yeah, after three beers maybe," said Lou.

"Sometimes it takes three beers for a person, to be honest," countered his cousin.

~~~

Twenty-six months later after seven-days-a-week training, high-security clearance, fifteen pounds lighter and with stomach ripped, Lou Slezak boarded the shuttle, SpaceArrow and eight months later, stepped onto Earth's pride and joy – the space station orbiting Jupiter's moon, Ganymede.

It was what he'd been led to expect after countless virtual tours, but at the same time was different. The tours had left out the odours and sounds, the sense of hustle and bustle and general joyful excitement. Most everyone he passed looked delighted to be there and strutted with purpose and self-importance. Down to the waiters and maintenance men, everyone *knew* what he or she was – an incredible explorer doing something that no human had done before – living in a civilization, albeit a small one of some five thousand souls, in a hopefully self-maintaining, artificial world.

But Lou didn't learn until a month after his arrival what the real purpose of Ganymede Station was. He and Simpson, head Waterworks Engineer, were looking at a segment of pipes under Entertainment, the section that housed eating establishments, two cinemas, holo-rooms, a spa and gym.

"There's a leak here somewhere," said Simpson. "Signal went off fifteen minutes ago. Not big, but humidity is slightly too high so we don't need an iota more H_2O loose. I'll check red level, you take yellow. Got your sensor? I know you were sawing wood when I buzzed you."

"Got it," said Lou. Yes, he'd been sleeping, but it was still all so new that any task thrilled him.

"You know you're the best out of all of them," said Simpson. "They may have their MIT educations, but I saw right off that you're a waterworks whisperer." He laughed. He was a short, wiry guy with chocolate brown skin and glowing teeth.

"You're embarrassing me," laughed Lou from his almost upside-down position. "Here's the leak. It looks like some kind of corrosion."

Simpson was down there in one second flat. He was like a hyperactive acrobat. "Shit," he said. He pressed his communicator and barked into it. "Turn off P section, Pod 17, NOW." To Lou, he said, "What could corrode plastic? Get a sample. We should have done the whole shebang in stainless steel, but you know government contracts. At least this is the only section."

"Sample," said Lou, handing Simpson a small tube. "I don't think the problem's too serious. Looks like some kind of motor oil. Apparently coming from up there." He pointed.

"Gravity Spin," said Simpson. "Anything goes wrong with that and we'll be pissing in the air." He pressed his communicator again. "Send Dubois down now. I don't care if his tummy *is* upset, just get him down here!"

While they waited, Lou said, "So are you ever going to tell me why they did build this station?"

"I'm going to open your mind," said Simpson, "but don't say you heard it from me because I'll deny it. Ten years ago, representatives from the EU, US and China convened in Switzerland in an underground facility where they received a message from a delegation of extraterrestrials from Proxima Centauri. I don't know exactly how the message was delivered, but however it was, it was believable and the representatives had no doubt that the senders meant business."

"What did they want?"

"They said they'd been monitoring our technological development and they were aware of our being on the edge of serious space exploration. They have or had a base on the dark side of the moon and keep a watch on the Mars settlement, struggling though it may be. They offered their assistance with further space advancement but said that to earn it, we would need to do more than the Mars thing which, as everyone knows, has not panned out all that well."

"Holy shit," said Lou. His mind was racing. "And 'more' is Ganymede Station?"

"You got it. This is the assignment. We're here."

"But . . . but why did we hear nothing about this on the news?"

Simpson chuckled. "Do you actually imagine the powers-that-be would officially admit to the general populace that space aliens have been watching them for decades or even centuries and that now these aliens want to contact and then allow this same populace to decide the response?"

Lou was going to reply when he stopped to examine his own emotions. There was no way around it — it was fear, mixed with excitement, but fear nonetheless. "I don't know," he finally said. "Some people would go nuts, but others would just accept it and still others would love it. You know, sci-fi aficionados and all."

Simpson shook his head. "I don't think it would go so smoothly. Not with the types who don't accept space travel in the first place – you know, it's against God or it's again nature, whatever. They can cause trouble."

"Wow," said Lou.

"Change of subject," warned Simpson. "Here comes Dubois."

~~~

What Simpson said turned out to be true – faster than anyone outside the upper echelons of Intel could have imagined. The station buzzed with the news, undoubtedly most of it about as accurate as preteen sex advice.

Lou, his cheeks flushed more than usual, sat on a bar stool at Zebang's talking to the attractive assistant manager, Zeenie Welsh. Behind her was a wide window into the black of space or the face of Jupiter, depending on which way the station happened to be turning as it revolved around Ganymede.

Zeenie was short, athletic-looking and down-to-business; she appeared capable of kicking ass if she had to. This was something Lou had not particularly noticed until Simpson had raised his consciousness about her possibly being undercover police.

"Do you think it's true?" he ventured. Now he felt he might have to censor anything he said outside of regular come-ons when and if he got to that. And speaking about the aliens, he knew his nervousness was obvious.

"The aliens?" she said. "Of course. They're on their way. You have the honour of being part of the first group of the humans to meet beings from another planet. Frankly, I'm excited as hell."

He looked at her. "Did you know when you signed on that this is what you'd be seeing?"

She hesitated and he knew instantly – Simpson was right. "It was on a need to know basis," she said, not looking into his eyes.

Lou could not resist giving her a knowing smile. When she didn't return it, he understood that she was all "secret cop" and for a while, this would dampen his romantic interest. Why, it was hard to say, but imagining the object of his affections as on-the-inside police was not conducive to masculine, amorous fantasies. Aside from that, was she dangerous? Was she working for good or bad people?

He seemed to hear his grandmother's voice in his head. Half Polish and half Romanian, she had claimed to be psychic and considerable evidence had backed up her stories. "Turn off your head," she had instructed him, "and listen only to your gut." She had poked him in his solar plexus. "Right there, kiddo, that is the radio receiver. Trust it."

When he tried to do that about Zeenie now, nothing negative came in, but maybe he didn't have his grandmother's talent.

But he couldn't stop wondering to whom she reported? Commissioner Jon Fasset was head of the station police force, but if she worked for him, why would she be undercover? Fasset's underlings on the station were out in the open and uniformed.

Simpson, once Lou managed to get him alone, had only vague speculations. "Politics," he mumbled.

"What do you mean exactly?"

"I don't know, maybe some groups back on Earth have spies in here."

"What groups and what for?"

Simpson shrugged. "Hey, I'm an engineer. I don't get involved in that stuff unless it affects me directly."

Frustrated, Lou returned to his work in Section Medical where a small area wasn't getting enough hot water. His emotions were a mishmash. Not only with the police suddenly strutting all over the place, but from his observation of the general excitement level of the residents, it was pretty obvious that the aliens were about to arrive. His speculations were shown to be accurate when later that day, Simpson called him to his office.

His friend was pacing, a clear indication of his own emotional state. "Lou, we've been called to special duty. Two suites in the elite residential section are going to be our areas of concentration. This would be two of the four set aside for bigwig visits. Check to see that everything is working perfectly. Water temp, pressure, heating, cooling, the works. My orders are to move up the temp, make it 27 °C. I guess they'll have to borrow sweaters if they are cold. Assuming they don't have twelve arms and fourteen legs."

That kind of thought haunted Lou too. "I don't like to admit it," he said, "but I'm apprehensive. What if their intentions aren't so friendly? What if they blow us up or something? You know, like on their way to Earth to finish that off too? Might not give us time to warn them at home. I have family back there."

"Don't we all," said Simpson. "Everything you're thinking, ditto."

In two days, an announcement was broadcast over the entire station. Everyone from top officials to the cleaning staff stopped to listen.

"Ganymede Residents: tomorrow at ten hundred hours, Ganymede station will host a landing for a small ship of visitors from another star system, Proxima Centauri. They call themselves Trevula. Apparently that is singular and plural. It is our job to welcome them and spend some days with them here before it can be determined if they and Earth want to meet. Some of you on the station may not come in contact with them, while others will. This may be a tense meeting or it may be quite pleasant, no one knows. This is a first for humankind and you all will go down in history for being part of it."

The next day passed without Lou or Simpson getting so much as a glimpse of the aliens and anything they could glean about them was only through stories flitting through the station.

"They're seven feet tall and sort of like us but not quite," said one man in the cafeteria. He was so excited that his hands caused his tray to shake. "I saw them from the lift before the doors closed."

"Their skin is very pale," said a woman nearby. "Almost translucent."

"Creepy eyes," said a counsellor from Medical. "Sort of colourless, and the pupils seem weird. I didn't get a long enough look but I don't think they're round."

"That silver hair is reasonably attractive," said the first women. "But so pale, they must live underground or somewhere without much sunlight."

"So they look pretty much human then?" said Lou with exasperation.

"Yes and no," said the counsellor. "You need to see for yourself."

"But how——" Lou was stopped by the reverberation of a faint explosion. It sounded as if it were coming from Section Science. Not bothering to say goodbye to anyone, he sprinted from the cafeteria to the nearest lift as he called for Simpson on his communicator.

"Section 9B!" Simpson yelled when Lou found him. "Get your gear, we're going to investigate." He sent his men in all directions but kept Lou close. "I trust you," he said simply.

Though people in Section Science were doing their best to contain their panic, their faces were ashen and their speech subdued. Everyone on board knew that any kind of serious hole in the hull, which was several layers thick, would be disastrous, and should the gravity rotator stop, everything on the station would float in air. While sections were supposed to be prepared for such an occasion, people did grow lax about taking the simulated gravity for granted and allowed specimens, equipment and belongings to be scattered about, any of which could prove dangerous should gravity stop.

"What happened?" asked Lou.

Simpson handed him a gas mask. "Through here," he said.

They descended via a small porthole into the under-workings of the station. Smoke was everywhere, along with metal fragments and gobs of melted plastic. Steam hissed from a shattered pipe. Lou was on it immediately, and shouting orders in all directions while opening his gear bag, got it quickly stopped up. "This was no accident," he told Simpson.

Simpson had the station police there in a matter of minutes, including Commissioner Fasset himself. A tall, powerfully built man, Fasset commanded the space around him, causing everyone else to fade into the background.

"We need to talk," said Simpson, "and I want Lou with me. He knows the pipes."

With what Lou felt was reluctance, the Commissioner waved for them both to follow him into a small side room. After impatiently listening to Simpson, he told them firmly, "This could not be sabotage. I don't want to hear any more from either of you to that effect. In your report, you will simply state what you found without adding your opinions on what caused it."

The old zip up, thought Lou, but why? Shouldn't the Commissioner be interested in something as serious as someone trying to blow up the space station? Lou shot Simpson a look of astonishment, but Simpson widened his eyes to imply that they would discuss it later.

"But what if—?" Lou could not hold back.

"That is an order, plumber, or whatever you are," snapped Fasset as he exited the room, leaving the two men to look at each other.

"Maybe he wants to avoid panic?" suggested Simpson.

"Why isn't he putting guards everywhere? Why didn't he tell us to expect to work round the clock till we find out what's going on? If the next explosion penetrates the hull, we—"

"You don't have to spell it out," interrupted Simpson. "I sure as hell don't want to die that way."

Fear gnawed at Lou in a way he had never before experienced. It stayed with him hard as he and his crew finished repairing the damages, which was not easy. A piece of metal was found embedded in the hull, a mere five and a half centimetres from the outside and potential disaster. The under-workings of the huge wheel of the station were divided into ten-meter pods, each closed off from the next so that should the hull be breached, the affected pod would not necessarily endanger the rest. For anyone working in an affected pod at the time, his life could hang by a thread. And if a larger explosion were involved, it could rip into other pods and possibly cause a chain reaction.

"Fasset *was* amazingly nonchalant," said Simpson.

"I'm *hoping* it's just because he just doesn't show emotion – military type and all," said Lou. "Because if that's not the reason, we have a bigger problem than we thought."

"I don't know," said Simpson, "but somebody had better find out who did this."

An announcement blasted through the station. "The Trevula will be making an appearance in four gathering places this evening, starting with Assembly One at 18:00, Assembly Two at 18:30, Glenn Cafeteria at 19:00 and Zebang's at 19:30. If you want to attend, sign up in front of Centre by 14:00. There is limited room."

Lou and Simpson were seated in Assembly One when two of the Trevula, flanked by a police escort, entered the small stage and stood by a podium. Lou felt his heart stop. While he knew intellectually what he was seeing, still he could barely believe his eyes. They looked almost human, but there were subtle differences. He wasn't sure he could breathe.

Next to him, in spite of the enormity of the occasion, Simpson had his head down, madly checking his communicator. Lou nudged him hard.

The moment that one very tall and pale Trevula stepped behind the podium and opened his (or her) mouth to speak, Simpson jumped from his seat, grabbed Lou and motioned for them to exit. Simpson hit the ground running.

What the hell, thought Lou, barely keeping up as their feet clanged against the metal floors. By the first lift, Simpson barked, "Pod 29C. Patel thought he saw someone unauthorized go in there!"

Pressing security codes into the lift panel, they flashed clearance colours from their lapels and shot past other waiting parties. Once the lift stopped, Simpson security-opened another panel inside the car and the two men climbed into a container. Closing the wall behind them, they shot off horizontally under the station floor to the designated section.

Simpson, about to call for police backup, was stopped by Lou's hand on his arm. "I don't know about that," he said.

"What do you mean?"

"Just this feeling." Was this what his grandmother had meant? "I'll go inside. Cover me."

"What are you talking about? How would I cover you? And what weapon would you have?"

"I'm a black belt in karate," said Lou.

Simpson laughed.

"Seriously."

"A lot of good that'll do against some military type saboteur. We'll both go. At least I have a regulation stun. I do not, though, have my equipment. No gas masks."

With heart thudding, Lou, with Simpson following, entered 29C and heard it close behind them. *Is this how I'm going to end?* thought Lou, close to panic. He made a Herculean effort and pushed the fear down, at least enough for him to function.

The lighting was dim. At first they saw no one, then Lou touched Simpson and jerked his head. Behind a tangle of pipes moved something black, which soon revealed itself to be a medium height, muscular figure. Simpson's stun shot out and the figure collapsed.

"Hit him again!" yelled Lou, but Simpson refrained. "I hit him hard; he'll be out for a good twenty minutes. I don't want to kill him."

Not sure about the wisdom of this choice, Lou moved to the spot where the figure had been hidden and yelled. "Bomb! It's set!"

Simpson spoke into his wrist, then grabbed Lou. "Let's get out of here!"

"Wait!" said Lou, intensely focused. "I recognize this. My brother worked bombs in the Arabian War. On his furlough, he spent most of his time in the garage, practising bomb deactivating and insisting on teaching me some of it. I hero-worshipped him, so I obeyed. This looks exactly like one he was working on. I remember him saying "third pin down".

"Are you crazy?" screamed Simpson. "Lou, please. I'm opening the hatch." He sounded on the edge of hysteria.

"If it goes off," said Lou, "the explosion will rip through these walls. Being in the hall won't matter. There will be nowhere safe."

Why was he feeling so strangely calm when a second ago he'd been sweating buckets? It was as if he were operating inside a glass bubble, cut off from the outside world. Even Simpson's yelling seemed muffled.

With the sangfroid of someone about to swat a fly, Lou reached up and pulled out pin number three. The infernal contraption stopped its quiet hum.

Simpson, who had been about to open the pod door, physically sagged with relief. "That piece of shit on the floor there," he said, jerking his head.

"Yeah," said Lou, who yanked plastic cord from a small wheel attached to his belt. "Let's hog tie him."

The man, still out cold, was heavy as a corpse, but together they managed to bind him into an extremely uncomfortable position.

Outside the door, someone pounded and a group of people yelled. Lou thought he heard Zeenie's voice, and finally the lock opening. How odd. Then suddenly, everything grew dim and he lost consciousness.

~~~

Some time later, he woke in Medical. Zeenie was sitting by his bed. As his blurry vision coalesced to reveal her beautiful face, he tried to make a joke but the effort cost him. "Tired," he muttered. Then after a pause, he said, "What was that gas? And how's Simpson?"

"The gas was a little add-on to try and kill anyone who disarmed the bomb."

"Simpson?" whispered Lou as loudly as he could.

Zeenie flushed and looked down. "He didn't make it," she said softly. "He was more sensitive to the gas than you were."

Lou choked and let out a sob.

She placed her hand on his arm. "Careful. You need to be gentle with your respiratory system." She paused. "He was a good man. He died a hero."

Lou couldn't respond.

"Lou," she said, "You and Simpson helped to save thousands of lives, including those of the Trevula. It was a miracle."

"The bomb?" he managed to whisper.

"It was an HMX bomb, high-quality military. How did you know how to disarm it?"

"Brother," said Lou. "His job once."

"It would have blown this station to bits. They tried putting it in one of the pods, thinking we'd be less likely to notice in time."

"We?"

She sighed. "Lou, I knew you suspected. International sent me along with a few others to work undercover. An extreme reactionary group was behind the sabotage, led by Commissioner Fasset. We figure there were four or more of them on the station, at least that's the number we've rounded up so far and the interrogations aren't over."

"But, what if—"

She pressed his shoulder gently. "Relax, we'll get them all. Suspects are being wired and injected. It all comes tumbling out."

I am going back home as soon as I can, Lou thought. *Without Simpson, this place is shit.*

In the end, he stayed, though he felt listless. They made him Head of Plumbing/Heating and immediately promoted someone to Head Engineer, who was nothing like Simpson, but a young, snot-nosed jerk.

Zeenie showed up at his door one night, wearing nothing under her uniform and they made the kind of love that people make when they know they probably won't see each other again. When she left the station the following day for her next assignment, Lou fell into a dangerous slump.

Shortly after, he ran into two Trevula as they entered an elevator with their silent police guards and a fast talking station rep who reminded Lou of a budding politician. Days before, he would have been anxious to be near the aliens, but his grief overpowered normal emotions. He tried to stand as far from the Trevula as he could in the small space and was startled when one of them reached out a long hand and touched his arm.

It was, he felt, a female though there was no way to know for certain. She/it said in her lilting accent, "Remain collected, friend. Your life will improve. You will know companions, you will experience love." She withdrew the hand and added, "We thank you." Her eyes with their water-like transparent colour and elongated pupils held his blue ones in a mental embrace.

Before he could respond, the lift stopped and the aliens exited. He was left alone to continue to his level.

The following day, President Lee transmitted all to the station. "We humans are not yet ready," he said. "If terrorism can happen here, imagine what could be waiting for the Trevula on Earth in spite of good intentions of the many. They are leaving later today and are not making any further contact. Commissioner Fasset won – not personally, of course, but on a much larger scale."

Lou felt deep sadness and embarrassment within him. He would find love of a personal nature, yes, but adventure of the sort he had begun to crave? Not in his lifetime.

MARGARET KARMAZIN's credits include stories published in literary and national magazines, including *Rosebud, Chrysalis Reader, North Atlantic Review, Mobius, Confrontation, Pennsylvania Review* and *Another Realm*. Her stories in *The MacGuffin, Eureka Literary Magazine, Licking River Review* and *Words of Wisdom* were nominated for Pushcart awards. Her story, "The Manly Thing," was nominated for the 2010 Million Writers Award. She has had stories included in *Still Going Strong, Ten Twisted Tales, Pieces of Eight (Autism Acceptance), Zero Gravity, Cover of Darkness, Daughters of Icarus, M-Brane Sci-Fi Quarterlies,* and a YA novel, *Replacing Fiona* and children's book, *Flick-Flick & Dreamer,* www.etreasurespublishing.com/pages/Margaret-Karmazin.html

Chances
Steve Jarratt

The room was purposefully stark and uninviting. Indoor smoking bans had been enforced too late to save the once cream-coloured walls and ceiling, now stained a sickly yellow. Attempts at cleaning graffiti had only resulted in angry smears. A single window of safety glass sat high on the wall behind slender bars, its opening long since painted shut. Only three of the four recessed lights glowed, and a defunct centre rosette marked where a lamp once dangled before its cord and glass became the tools of the desperate. The furniture – a table and three chairs – were practical to the point of ugliness. Formal, synthetic, bland; indifference made solid. If rooms could talk, this one would probably say, "Kill me."

The single door of plain pine veneer was guarded by tall, stocky man; expressionless, arms folded. Regulation black trousers, short-sleeved shirt, and peaked cap marked him out as a member of the local Police Department; blue lettering on his silver oval badge narrowed it down to Los Angeles.

The table lay at an odd angle in the centre of the room. On the side nearest the door sat a man and woman, both in formal attire. The man, a detective, slouched in the lower half of a wrinkled, dark grey suit – its jacket slung over the chair so his shoulder holster and standard issue Glock .22 were clearly on display. His shirt – at least one size too small – was equally wrinkled and showing the first signs of staining around the neck. The sleeves were rolled up to reveal huge forearms, and the stitching strained against the bulk of his shoulders. He'd played defensive tackle for his college football team until he discovered drink and girls. Too many donuts and too little cartilage meant he couldn't run any more, but his bulk came in useful for shaking down the junkie scumbags that inhabited his precinct.

The woman, a police psychologist just on the wrong side of 40, wore a dark blue jacket and skirt, with a pale frilled blouse. Unflattering glasses, tied-up hair and minimal makeup were a self-imposed attempt to lessen her allure. A career girl, she wanted to be taken seriously, not just seen as some 'piece of ass shrink' – though most of the cops would have told her not to bother. She sat with a pad and pen, making preparatory notes, because that's what you do when you're serious about your job.

Opposite them sat a man with an aura of confidence; a demeanour just on the right side of smug. He was dressed smart-casual, but his jeans cost more than the detective made in a month, his watch as much as the beat cop made in a year. A youthful complexion and thick head of hair belied his 30-odd years. Clear blue eyes looked on calmly, and his lips bore the slightest hint of a smile. He sat, hands on the table, fingers interlocked.

Gripping the pad to her chest with one hand, the woman fumbled in her bag to reveal a small silver voice recorder. She clicked a button, leaned over and placed it on the table, end up. "LA Police Wilshire Area, detention room 4. August 8th, 2015. Case NR17498FD, Suspect William Devon. Present is LAPD Detective Malcolm—"

"It's Mal," growled the cop. Only his mom and his ex called him 'Malcolm'.

"Detective Mal Gorr and psychoanalyst Christine Peters."

The detective took a deep breath and stared at his suspect. "So, Devon, here we are again. For the benefit of Peters here, would you mind telling us a bit about yourself?"

"Sure," said Devon, politely. "My name is William Grant Devon. I'm an IT consultant working on enterprise communications for LA County – or, at least I was."

"You quit?" asked Gorr.

"Yeah, just over a month ago. I didn't think it was really necessary given my, uh . . . new skillset, shall we say."

"IT specialist, eh?" The corners of Gorr's mouth, turned downwards, Robert de Niro-style. "Must have been a pretty tasty number."

"I did okay," said Devon, nodding. "Pulled down about sixty thousand a year."

"So can you explain to us how you ended up with . . ." Gorr took a scruffy pad from his shirt pocket and checked his notes. ". . . eight point two million dollars held in four separate accounts. And . . ." Gorr flipped his pad. ". . . while you're at it, perhaps you could also shed some light on the disappearance of one Michael K. Flanagan, formerly of the Crystal Casino and Hotel, and three of his associates."

Devon looked him in the eye, and then glanced at Peters. "It's pretty much as I told you before, Detective Gorr."

"Well you have a new audience," said Gorr hooking a thumb at Peters, "so tell us again."

Devon raised his eyebrows and sighed. "Okay, Miss Peters. I appreciate why you've been brought in on the case. So you get the long version."

Gorr rolled his eyes and groaned.

"It all began with dice," he said, matter-of-factly. "I used to play board games with friends – y'know, basic stuff. A bit of Risk, some strategy games from Europe. Me and the guys would get together and play games, eat pizza and drink beer. Good times." His smile widened at the memory.

Devon paused momentarily, regarding his two interrogators. "Have you ever had the feeling that you know exactly what's going to happen, the split second before it actually occurs?"

The pair remained silent. Devon shrugged almost imperceptibly and continued. "I had it. All the time. Even when the dice rolls were ridiculous – like, someone would roll one dice against my three, and even though the odds were stacked against them, I knew I'd lose. And it kept happening . . . sometimes a win, sometimes a loss. It was freaking me out."

He paused and stroked his lips with one hand. "And then it dawned on me: instead of just predicting these dice rolls, maybe it was me making them happen."

Detective Gorr raised his eyebrows and made a low grunting noise. "See Peters, this is why I requested your, uh, expertise in the matter."

Peters looked straight ahead. "Can you elucidate please, Mr Devon."

"Of course, ah, Christine, isn't it?"

"That's Mrs Peters to you," snapped Gorr, leaning forward and tapping his index finger on the table.

"Actually, it's Miss."

The detective exhaled noisily, and sat back, folding his arms again.

Devon glanced at them in turn. "I'm not talking about ESP or telekinesis or any of that rubbish." He batted the idea away with his hand. "Are you familiar with the notion of the multiverse? It's a scientifically valid theory, which suggests that there are an infinite number of realities all happening concurrently – we're just experiencing one of them at any given moment."

"Are you talking about parallel universes?" asked Peters.

"Yeah, sort of," replied Devon, nodding. "The theory basically states that everything that *can* happen, already has – we just haven't experienced it yet. Every time we make a decision we enter a different universe, like when you decide to turn left or turn right. Our actions determine which of the many potential universes we pass through, but we have only the most basic influence over the outcome."

He sat back in his chair, rubbing the first signs of stubble. "Well, anyway, it turns out that the theory is true. The majority of people drift through these realities like a leaf on the surface of a stream, just going with the flow. But me, I'm like a fish, able to swim in any direction I want."

Peters sat upright, frowning. "But how can you possibly have any direct control over these events?"

"Ah, now that I don't really understand," said Devon, grinning. "But I've always thought that the power of the mind was vastly misunderstood. After all, the brain generates electric impulses, magnetic fields, it's our connection to the universe." He glanced at Gorr, who was idly examining his fingernails. "Or not, in some cases."

Peters suppressed a smile. "Go on."

"I started to believe that instead of having déjà vu or something, I was actually influencing the outcome of the dice rolls. If I was feeling negative, the outcome would go against me, like I was being self-destructive – and vice versa. So I started to practice, trying to keep a positive attitude and forcing the results I wanted. Eventually I got the hang of it. Remember, I'm not changing the universe, just the path I take through it. For example, whenever a dice is rolled, there are six possible results, six possible routes to alternate realities. I merely decide which direction to go in."

Gorr unfolded his arms, resting their huge bulk on the table. "Christ Devon, where is this fantasy of yours leading? It's gonna be a real long day if you keep stringing us along with these stories. Might I remind you that this is a police investigation into fraud and multiple homicide, not an interview with the National Enquirer." He glanced sideways. "You, too, Peters."

The woman shot him a look. She didn't much care for this brutish cop, and the man in front of her, while clearly delusional, made a pleasant change from the usual low-level psychopaths. "Detective Gorr, you brought me here to analyse your suspect," she said pointedly. "Now if you'll kindly let me do my job . . . ?"

Gorr harrumphed and went back to finding something fascinating about his fingers.

Peters turned back to Devon. "Continue, please."

"Well, after a while, I was getting a really high hit rate, which is when I decided to try my luck in the casinos. As you can see from my bank statements, the experiment turned out rather well." He glanced at the detective. "And there's nothing illegal about holding substantial amounts of money in regular checking accounts, Mr Gorr."

The detective tapped the table again. "So why split it across four different banks?"

Devon looked sheepish. "Ah, well I was, somewhat naively, trying to not draw attention to myself. I thought earning over eight million in just over six months might be rather . . . suspicious?"

"Ha!" barked Gorr. "You call gambling 'earning'?"

"So you admit that my unorthodox system is real? That I did actually win it by gambling?"

Gorr frowned. "I don't know how you did it, pal, probably some cheap math trick. But I know the casinos weren't best pleased with your antics. They got to talking and I guess Flanagan and his cronies paid you a visit? And that's when you took 'em out, right?"

Devon chuckled. "What, a 160-pound IT specialist fought and killed a mobster and his three heavies. *Really*?"

Gorr leaned forward. "Well, they were last seen departing the casino, about five minutes after you left having just relieved them of six-hundred grand. We have the CCTV footage. They ain't been seen since."

"Perhaps they went on a 'bromantic' road trip?" Devon added quotation marks with his fingers.

Peters quickly reached over and placed a hand on Gorr's arm just as he was gearing up for an argument. "Please, may we continue with the interview?"

Gorr slowly settled back in his chair, glaring.

Devon looked directly at the woman. "The truth is, lots of people do what I do, but just don't know it. Politicians, CEOs, natural born leaders. Those with a strong will can forge their own path; likewise the meek and weak-willed are content to be wafted along on the cosmic tides. Look at Steve Jobs: now there was a man who navigated the universe to suit his own ends. People even referred to his 'reality distortion field' – if only they knew how close they were."

"So how far can you go?" said Peters, colluding with the man's fantasy. "I mean . . . what do you think you're capable of?"

"Unfortunately, there's still logic to the universe," said Devon, tilting his head and looking thoughtful. "Changing the roll of a dice to a six is only a small step away from the reality we're currently in. You're still limited by the laws of chance and probabilities."

"So rolling two sixes in succession takes more effort?" said Peters.

Devon pointing a cocked finger in her direction. "Exactly."

"How many consecutive sixes can you roll?" asked Peters.

"Nineteen. And then I passed out. I was sick for two days."

Peter's stared into the man's eyes. There was the briefest glimpse of pain at the recollection. Either he was a consummate liar, or had become a slave to his own imaginings.

"So you couldn't, for example, turn Detective Gorr into a frog?"

Gorr snorted. "What about making casino bosses and their minions disappear?"

"No," replied Devon. "I can't subvert the laws of nature or physics. Or make things happen that wouldn't ordinarily occur. But then, most of the time, you don't need to."

The lightness of Devon's demeanour began to fade: his slight smile remained, but his eyes grew cold. "I can't make people vanish into thin air. But I can steer them out of my way, onto a path of my choosing. For example, what are the chances of a slow-witted mobster on a diet of junk food and cocaine failing to make a turn when driving too fast?"

The room fell quiet. Peters stole a glimpse at Gorr, who looked on, unblinking.

Devon pouted slightly, his shoulders raised. "I'd say those chances were pretty high. You know La Sierra, that twisting road that runs along Lake Matthews?"

Blank faces.

"Well if I were you, I'd try searching there. Although you might need some Scuba gear."

Gorr sat upright. "This is bullshit, Devon. You're living in a dream world." His chair scraped the floor as he stood up. "I need a break." He walked to the cop on guard at the door. "Keep an eye on these two," he snarled, before looking back at his suspect, scowling. He flung the door open and strode out.

Peters looked back, surprised at the detective's sudden exit. She smoothed the material on her skirt, coughed, and needlessly checked the voice recorder before deciding to make a few notes.

"Do I make you nervous?" asked Devon.

Peters continued writing for a moment, before looking up. "Not at all, Mr Devon."

"Please, call me Will."

"Mr Devon, we're here for the investigation of some very serious matters. These fantastical stories of yours are only going to serve to annoy the police and harm your cause – on the assumption that you are indeed innocent until proven otherwise."

"But you believe me. Don't you?"

She placed her pad on the table and laid the pen on top. She cocked her head slightly to one side. "I believe that you think you can alter your own fate – be it wish-fulfilment, an innate desire to succeed, a mild egocentric psychosis . . . But has it not occurred to you that all these events may well be coincidence? That what you think is under your control is actually just the natural order of things, and you're subconsciously altering your perception to suit your own needs?"

Devon looked back, impassive, but breathing heavily. Peters saw his jaw muscles tighten. After a moment's pause, he grabbed the pad and scribbled something, then tore the page out. He folded the paper up and slid the pad back to Peters.

"What's your favourite colour?" he said, more of an order than a question.

Peters had to stop and think. "It's . . . blue"

"Any particular shade?"

Again, she paused to consider it. "Er . . . Navy. Navy blue."

Frowning, Devon tossed the paper towards her. She looked up at him; he was pale and his brow was dotted with sweat. He suddenly looked tired. Peters started to feel a sense of cold dread, a growing anxiety of what was about to take place. Trembling hands slowly unfolded the sheet. It read: 'The voice recorder has gone'.

She looked up to where her voice recorder was – or rather, had been. It was, indeed, gone. In its place was a standard police issue, old-school cassette deck, battered and near the end of its useful life. She felt the blood draining from her face. The coldness enveloped her; it was starting to feel very much like fear.

"What are the chances of you forgetting to bring your voice recorder today?"

"But it was there – I took it from my bag, and placed it . . ."

"You see Christine, I just switched to an alternate timeline in which you forgot to pack your voice recorder. It was more effort than I thought," he said, wiping his brow. "I suspect you're not the kind of person that forgets things easily."

Peters rummaged in her bag and searched under the table. She looked back at the cop guarding the door, who had long given up eavesdropping and was thinking about his date this evening with the hot girl from the coffee shop. Peters started to mouth a question but decided against it.

She felt dizzy and confused and could feel her eyes beginning to water. She thought for a moment. "But I remember bringing the recorder. If . . . if you've taken a new path, how come I'm here?"

Devon looked at her. She had the same expression you see on people after an accident or receiving news of a death in the family. The wide-eyed stare; a mind scrambling to find reason in the chaos.

"I don't really know," he said quietly. "Inertia? Some shared neural connections? People in my vicinity seem to get dragged along for a while, like a leaf caught up in my wake. It passes."

"Goddamn it!" Gorr burst back in, knocking the guard to one side. He banged his fists on the table. "How did you do it, Devon. You cut the brake hose? Leave a stinger on the road?"

Peters looked up, a handkerchief pressed to one eye. "What . . . what is it?"

"I just checked with traffic. They found a break in the barriers along La Sierra, and tyre marks. We're getting a search team over there right now."

"Don't forget the aqualungs," said Devon, a wry smile on his lips.

Peters grabbed Gorr's arm. "The recorder . . ."

Caught off guard, Gorr stopped mid-rant and looked down, a puzzled look on his reddening face. "What – has it stopped working? Sorry, kiddo, that's the best we could do at short notice."

Her grip gradually loosened. "Yes . . . of course," she said, her mind slowly aligning itself to this new reality. She smiled thinly. "I'm getting forgetful in my old age." She remembered now, picturing it stood on the breakfast bar. She'd left it there while searching for new batteries.

Leaning forward, Gorr loomed over his suspect. He could smell a kill. "You're going down, Devon. As soon as we can link you to this accident – and we will – you'll be on a charge for multiple homicide. Voluntary manslaughter at worst. You've just given me probable cause, so you'll be spending another night in the cells."

Devon looked up, steely-eyed. "I don't think so."

Gorr took a step back. An abrupt feeling of nausea came over him. He felt light-headed; better sit down. He dragged the chair back and flopped his bulk onto its bare wooden seat.

"You're over 50," said Devon darkly. "You drink too much, smoke cigars and eat too many TV dinners. What are the chances of a blood clot forming in your arteries?"

Gorr rubbed his chest, which was beginning to grow tight. His face grew pale and he was starting to sweat. All he could do was glare at Devon through squinted eyes.

Worried, Peters stood and put a hand on Gorr's huge shoulder. "What's the matter? Are you okay?" She turned to the beat cop. "You – go get help. We need a medic. Now!" Without saying a word, the officer obediently turned and flew out of the room, slamming the door behind him.

Devon stood up, wearily. He brushed away some imagined dust from his jacket sleeves and pulled down the hem. "Well this little exercise has been fun, but now I really have to go," he said to no one in particular. He tugged at his shirt collar and started towards the door.

Peters mopped Gorr's brow with her handkerchief and tried to loosen his shirt. She glanced up, her face furrowed with confusion. "Where the hell are you going?"

"I'm going home," said Devon, casually.

"But you're in a police station. You'll never get out."

"A small fire has just started in all the waste paper out back," said Devon tilting his head towards the window. "It will rapidly spread to the main offices, and in all the confusion, I shall simply stroll out of the main door. Sadly, all the paperwork and computer files regarding my arrest will be destroyed."

"What about him?" She nodded to Gorr who was wincing at the pain in his chest and arms.

Devon made the tiniest of shrugs. "He'll live." Then he paused, staring her in the eyes. "For now."

The implied threat wasn't lost on the psychoanalyst. "You . . . you did this?" her tone a mixture of accusation and disbelief.

Devon glanced around the room, glad to be almost free of its oppressive gloom. He should never have been arrested, but they'd caught him unawares, tired and hung over, unable to alter the chain of events that led him here. He'd be more careful next time.

"You're a monster," she spat, a look of contempt on her face.

"No, Miss Peters." Devon opened the door, just as alarm bells started to ring. He looked out on the mayhem, and smiled. "I am a god."

102

STEVE JARRATT completed a Chemistry degree before he bluffed his way into videogame journalism, and enjoyed a successful career in the '80s and '90s, creating magazines such as *Commodore Format, Total!* and *Edge*. He launched several other titles, including technology magazine *T3*, but now works as a freelance journalist, editorial trainer and CG artist. He is indebted to the members of the small writing/drinking group, who inspired him to begin writing short stories.

Commemoration of the Faithful Departed

Steve Pease

Ask any established businessman to list his chief bugbears. Chances are he'll include accounting, invoicing, and logistics. The devil, of course, is in the detail. How do you calculate and bring in what is due? How do you manage the flow of goods between the point of origin and the point of consumption?

Over several board meetings, we concluded that we had a real problem.

"More and more of our stakeholders are losing faith," I argued. "They can see that our systems are a shambles. Key-product delivery is often late, and frequently early, but it's rarely on time."

"It's a hellish mess," agreed my business partner. "Lots of people settle minor accounts in advance, but most of our heavy debtors are deaf to encouragement, reminders and warnings – months and years pass before they pay up."

The very foundations of our business were rocking, and we were desperate for a road to redemption. Which is probably why we fell for the marketing spiel.

The company we brought in promised salvation.

"We are global thought-leaders," they affirmed. "And we'll push the envelope, harvesting knowledge, to leverage your competitive advantage and introduce market-leading process velocity."

My partner and I didn't understand a word, but – foolishly – we bought it. And here's what happened:

- wall-to-wall dark suits;
- condescension and platitudes;
- off-the-shelf solutions that had no place, or hope, in our business.

All delivered by consultants that seemed like 12-year-old kids to our eyes.

After six months, grinning like the self-satisfied offspring of The Cheshire Cat, they showed us a PowerPoint slide:

- A new IT program
- Containing 30/30/30 smart-system algorithms

- That will support payment price prioritisation
- With automated links to a dedicated 'no nonsense, no exceptions, no excuses' enforcement team
- Triggering robust action to ensure prompt payment.

(Let me explain in layman's terms. All major debts and credits would be settled within thirty days, interim values within thirty weeks, and minor accounts would enjoy up to thirty years grace).

When you've been in business as long as I have, you've witnessed more than your share of unjust or disastrous outcomes. Time after time, I've seen the criminally corrupt emerge triumphant, whilst the honest brokers end up bloodied and beaten. So maybe I should have been prepared for what happened next.

System development over-ran, and, consequently, user acceptance testing was sacrificed. The planned 'go-live' date of the first of January slipped by some ten months. And that's when I really should have seen trouble coming. But, despite what you might think, omnipotence is not an exact science.

See, I'd always thought of the second of November as The Commemoration of the Faithful Departed. It was only when I pressed the button, and chaos ensued, that I remembered it's also called All Souls' Day. The prioritisation algorithms were useless, but enforcement was one hundred per cent perfect.

Everyone was invoiced simultaneously. Every account got settled immediately. Every soul turned up together.

The usual soundtrack to my existence has been happy voices as long-lost friends are reunited, a blast of trumpets as lovers kiss again, the thump, thump, thump as the tails of childhood dogs greet again their once young owners. But today, for the first time in the millennia since my partner and I argued and made the company a two-site business, I heard raised voices on my floor.

Going out to investigate, I found a greying couple in heated argument. You'd have thought he'd be happy; finishing off his chef-prepared gourmet lunch, before a round on his private golf course with his lifelong best friends. Instead, I heard him berating his wife: "You and your fruit and fibre,

106

your damned Pilates and yoga. Stop smoking, drink less. Without your interference, I could have been here years ago."

My partner's suffering worse. In his department, he's got imp-shortages on the fuel supply lines. And demons working double shifts, trying to separate squabbling bankers, politicians and paedophiles – each arguing the others should be first in line for the pits, and thus burn the longest. (Tough call for Lucifer, that one. I don't envy him).

What I've learned from all of this is that outsiders can never know your business as well as you do yourself. Now I just have to figure out how we switch our old accrual system back on.

And if I'm ever tempted to dabble in that creation thing again, rest assured I'll be wasting none of day six making consultants.

STEVE PEASE once had a 'proper job', drafting press releases and briefings for British politicians. He argues, rather convincingly, that this was an ideal apprenticeship in the realms of fantasy. These days, he enjoys an idyllic lifestyle – walking his dogs by the River Derwent in Yorkshire, and dreaming up ideas for his twin passions of story and songwriting. "Commemoration of the Faithfull Departed" is his first published work, and he tips his hat in thanks to his good friend – World Fantasy Award-winning U.S. author, Lewis Shiner – whose abiding encouragement and advice have helped enable this breakthrough.

THE
SINGULARITY

The Singularity is a new SF and fantasy fiction magazine,
based in London, England, that publishes short fiction that is
singular in voice and style.

www.thesingularitymagazine.com

Made in the USA
Middletown, DE
05 February 2016